Note to Readers

While the Allertons and Foys are fictional families, many of the events you will read about in this book actually happened. In 1721, Boston had a terrible smallpox epidemic, and hundreds of people died. The Rev. Cotton Mather encouraged people to receive experimental inoculations, but many doctors opposed the unproven treatment. Germs hadn't been discovered yet, and no one understood the ideas of immune systems or antibodies.

People were afraid that Cotton Mather was trying to spread the disease. They became so angry that someone actually tried to blow up the Mather home with a bomb.

Ben Franklin, who appears in this story, actually was a young apprentice in Boston at this time and worked for his brother James. He later wrote about how much he hated working in James's print shop, and as soon as he could, he left Boston for Philadelphia.

After the smallpox epidemic ended, studies showed that the experimental inoculations saved many people from ever getting the disease. These crude injections of live pus eventually developed into smallpox vaccinations.

The American Adventure

SMALLPOX STRIKES!

Norma Jean Lutz

BARBOUR
PUBLISHING, INC.
Uhrichsville, Ohio

© MCMXCVII by Barbour Publishing, Inc.

ISBN 1-57748-144-5

Published by Barbour Publishing, Inc.
P.O. Box 719
Uhrichsville, Ohio 44683
http://www.barbourbooks.com

ecpa Member of the
Evangelical Christian
Publishers Association

Printed in the United States of America.

Cover illustration by Chris Cocozza.
Inside illustrations by Adam Wallenta.

CHAPTER ONE
Smallpox Strikes Boston

Eleven-year-old Robert Allerton leaned on his birch broom to rest for a moment. He'd swept out the offices at the far end of the counting house, and now he was almost finished with the main counting room. May sunshine streamed through an open window and a wasp drifted in and droned leisurely above his head. He watched it a moment.

"You're silly to be coming in here," Rob told the wasp. "If I were you, I'd stay outside where you can be free."

Rob stepped toward the window that faced Long Wharf and took a breath of the wonderful salt air coming in off Boston Harbor. Gulls cried and shrieked overhead as though they were directing all the busy activities on the wharves. A ship from Barbados in the West Indies had docked the night before. Shouts rang out as the sailors unloaded barrels, bales, and crates of merchandise from that distant island. Leaning farther out the window, he could get a better view of the twin-masted schooner.

"Master Robert," said a voice from behind him.

Rob spun around at the sound of his name. It was only Mr. Vetch, secretary to Rob's stepfather. "Good morning, sir. I didn't know anyone else had arrived."

"I thought as much." Mr. Vetch took his gold wire-rimmed spectacles from their case, hooked them over his ears, and adjusted them on his nose.

Rob was the first to arrive at the counting house of the Foy Shipping Line each morning. As his stepfather's youngest apprentice, it was his job to unlock the doors and make the rooms ready for the day's work.

"Is that birch broom doing a proper job of holding you up?" asked Mr. Vetch.

"I'm sweeping, sir."

"Not too much from the looks of it. Hadn't you better get the ink pots and sand jars filled before Mr. Goddard arrives?" Mr. Goddard was the chief clerk, and he didn't take kindly to loafers.

"Yes, sir," Rob answered. He hurried to the anteroom where supplies were stored. He propped the birch broom in the corner and took down the pitcher of ink. Carefully he filled the ink pots at each of the tall desks in the main counting room. Relieved that he'd managed to finish that task without spilling a drop of ink, Rob next poured the fine sand that would be used throughout the day for blotting the ink.

In a few months he, too, would be seated on the high stools where he would carefully record the business transactions of the shipping lines. Such a wearisome and dull occupation. He didn't look forward to that time at all.

Just as he returned the pitcher to the shelf, a tall boy stepped into the anteroom. "Good morning, Robert. Running late as usual, I see."

"I'm not late," Rob retorted quickly.

"You're always late. Either that or you're just plain slow." Noah was one of the older apprentices. He seemed to enjoy criticizing Rob's work. Noah and his coworker, Marcus, often played tricks on Rob, making him appear foolish. "Are the quills sharpened yet?"

"You can see with your own eyes, I'm getting ready to do that." Rob waved his jackknife in the air to prove the fact.

Noah reached his long arms up to lift down the heavy correspondence and accounting books from off the shelf. He was responsible for placing the books out on the desks. "It's about time," he said as he walked out the door.

Rob heaved a sigh and sat down on a stool in the corner and commenced to sharpen quills. He was never sure which job at the counting house he despised the most, but sharpening quills was certainly close. The anteroom was small and dark with no windows. At least with the arrival of spring it wasn't so cold. Now he no longer had to lay the fire in the fireplace or thaw frozen ink before beginning the day's work.

The pile of sharpened feather quills was growing. At last he gathered them up, placed them in a basket, and carried them out to the desks. First he headed toward the office of his stepfather, Josiah Foy, where he placed three new quills in the inkstand on the large cluttered desk. Next he placed three on Mr. Vetch's desk as well.

As he turned to go, he paused to listen. Just outside the door were voices. It was Noah speaking to Marcus. Evidently the boys had not seen Rob enter the office.

". . .Never on time and never completes a task properly," Noah was saying. Rob tiptoed nearer the door.

"It appears to me that he tries hard," came Marcus's reply.

"Tries? Why, he barely tries at all. He just takes up space. Ah, but then why should he? Being stepson to the owner allows him straight passage into one of these offices one day."

"Favor without responsibility. Is that your meaning?" asked Marcus.

"Exactly."

Rob ducked back out of the way just as the older boys passed by the door. Luckily he wasn't seen.

Throughout the long day, as he polished the brass doorknobs and scrubbed the front doorstep, the boys' words rang in his head. How could Noah think he was being favored? As far as Rob was concerned, life in the counting house wasn't much better than being locked in stocks in the town square.

Just before closing time, Mr. Vetch came to Rob with a rolled paper in hand. "Master Robert, you're to take this advertisement to the *Boston News Letter* office. Tell Mr. Campbell to put it on the Foy account."

Rob felt his heart leap. "Yes, sir," he said, taking the document and heading toward the front door.

"Master Robert?"

"Yes, Mr. Vetch?"

"Don't forget your hat and coat."

It was so warm, Rob had nearly forgotten. He grabbed his tricorn hat and blue woolen greatcoat and headed for the door. As he went out he heard Mr. Vetch say, "Mr. Foy says you may go straight home from the *News Letter* office."

"Yes, sir," he called back.

He dodged in and out of the traffic of two-wheeled carts and carriages moving along Long Wharf, then narrowly missed running smack into two British soldiers who were decked out in smart scarlet uniforms. "Hey, watch it there, young fellow," one called out. Rob never even glanced back. The entire wharf was piled high with barrels and bales of merchandise either being loaded on or unloaded off the many ships docked there.

Rain had fallen for many days during that April. The end of the dreary wet weather made Rob even more grateful for the warm sun. Leaving Long Wharf, he ran down King Street, turning at Washington, which was thick with mud. Outside the *News Letter* office, two pigs wallowed in the mud. They squealed and scrambled out of the way as Rob came toward them.

"Good afternoon, Mr. Campbell," Rob called as he stepped inside the print shop.

"Good afternoon to you, young man." Mr. Campbell was seated at the compositing bench. From the cases of metal type, he pulled out metal letters and placed them on the compositor's stick. Rob's friend Samuel Lankford often said that Mr. Campbell was the fastest compositor in all Boston. Without looking up from his work, he said, "I trust you've brought more business from the Foy Shipping Lines."

"That I have." Rob waved the paper in his hand. "Another advertisement. Mr. Vetch asked that you please place it on my stepfather's account."

"Josiah Foy's account is good as sterling at this place of business." Mr. Campbell laid down the finished row of typeset and stood to his feet. He was a stout fellow with a thick neck and graying wispy hair. "Let's see what you have there," he said.

Rob handed him the paper and followed him to a desk in the corner. "We'll have this in the next issue of the *News Letter*," Mr. Campbell said as he studied the sheet. "By the way, I have a letter here for your mother and Mr. Foy." The print shop also served as a local post station and Mr. Campbell as the postmaster. He reached into a pigeonhole of the desk and drew out a folded sheet that was sealed with wax. "Looks like it's from Mr. Foy's married sister in Roxbury."

Rob studied the swirls of the handwriting on the letter. "That's Aunt Esther's handwriting for sure. They'll be pleased to see this. Thank you. Now may I visit a moment with Sam? Is he here?"

Rob's friend Samuel Lankford served as an apprentice for Mr. Campbell and was usually there sweeping and cleaning. On occasion, Mr. Campbell even allowed him to set type.

"Sam's outside cooking up a fresh batch of ink." He waved his hand toward the back door. "See that you don't distract him for long."

"No, sir, I won't. Thank you, sir." He tucked the letter into the pocket of his silk waistcoat, replaced his tricorn hat on his head, and made his way through the maze of printing apparatus to the back.

At the door, Rob saw his friend stirring the mammoth kettle

filled with bubbling black ink. The greasy aroma filled the air. Sam was hatless, and the sunshine played on his golden-red hair and made his fair skin appear even lighter than usual. A leather apron covered his front to protect him from the black liquid.

"Is the soup done?" Rob called out.

Sam looked up and laughed. "Any soup that smelled this bad should be thrown out. What brings you out of the counting house?"

"The blessing of an errand. Mr. Vetch asked me to deliver an advertisement."

"Did Mr. Campbell tell you the latest news?"

Rob stepped nearer, cautiously studying the greasy liquid. "No, he didn't. What news?" Being in the newspaper office, Sam had firsthand information about everything that happened in Boston.

"A case of smallpox has been reported on the *Seahorse*."

"Isn't that the ship that just came in last night from Barbados?"

"That's the one."

Rob shivered. He'd heard many stories about the terrors of this horrible disease. Thankfully the *Seahorse* was not one of Josiah's ships. "Just one case?" Rob asked.

Sam nodded as he stirred with a large fat pole. "The trouble is, Captain Paxson allowed the man to come ashore to his home near the wharf."

"Isn't that dangerous?"

"I think it is. I guess he felt he needed to take care of the man. At any rate, the town selectmen are going to inspect the ship tomorrow. They'll find out if everything is as it should be."

Just then, Mr Campbell came to the door. "Enough chattering out there boys. You sound like a couple of old fishwives." The old man chuckled as he said it. He was a kind employer for Sam, and Rob was grateful that his friend enjoyed his position at the print shop. Rob was envious. How he wished he could enjoy his work at the counting house.

"I was just leaving, sir," Rob told him. He bade the two of them good-day and hurried out of town toward his home near Copp's Hill. Had Rob's mother, Mary, not married Josiah Foy, Rob might be living on the South End of Boston near Sam. Then the two of them could enjoy time together more often. As it was, Rob was a "North Ender," dressed in ruffles and silk, while Sam was a "South Ender," dressed in leather breeches and linsey-woolsey shirts.

As Rob neared the stately, white, two-story home on the hill, he heard the wailing of his little sister, Rachel. He quickened his steps through the gate of the picket fence, past the flower gardens, and around to the back orchard. The cries were louder. Through the trees he saw his younger stepbrother, Thomas, who appeared to be laughing.

"What is it, Thomas? What's the matter with Rachel?"

Thomas jumped back at the sound of Rob's voice. Rachel was sitting under an apple tree with a wounded, bleeding kitten in her lap. Her cries filled the air. For being only five, she could set up quite a noise.

"Thomas did it to Kitty," she cried out when she saw Rob. "He sicced a big old tomcat on her. He's mean."

The sight of little Rachel clutching the wounded kitten tugged at Rob's heart. He couldn't bear to see her crying. Without another thought he ran up to Thomas and gave him a mighty shove, landing him squarely in a mud puddle that shot up sprays of muddy water in all directions.

Now it was Thomas who was wailing. "You just wait until I tell Father what you've done," he yelled as he jumped up and ran to the house.

But Rob paid no mind. He reached down to lift Rachel to her feet. Pulling out his own silk shirttail, he created a cradle for the kitten.

"Put the kitten here, Rachel," he told her. Gently, she did as she was told. "Come with me, Rachel. We're taking your kitten to Dr. Boylston's apothecary shop."

Contradicts

CHAPTER TWO

Dr. Boylston Mends Matters

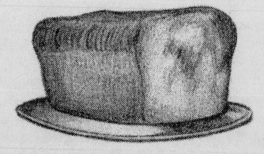

Rob knew full well he shouldn't have lashed out against his stepbrother. He knew his actions were wrong, but how he despised a bully. Thomas was nine, almost ten; he had no reason to hurt Rachel or her kitten. Rob took long strides as he led the way back down Salem Street to Hanover. Poor little Rachel was nearly running to catch up, sniffling all the way.

By the time they reached Dr. Boylston's shop, Rachel was quite out of breath. "Will Kitty be all right?" she asked in a high quivery voice.

"Doctor will know the answer to that." Rob slowed down then, realizing how fast he'd been walking. Cradling the kitten with one hand, he reached out to take Rachel's hand with the other. Her hand felt tiny and warm in his. "Mean old, mean old Thomas," he heard her muttering under her breath.

Dr. Boylston's shop was located past Faneuil Hall, next to the Feather Store in Dock Square. Rob hoped he was still there. Releasing Rachel's hand, he pushed against the big door.

It swung open. Pungent aromas of salves, ointments, and herbs filled the air. How Rob loved those interesting smells.

From the back room, Dr. Boylston suddenly appeared. Although the doctor was over fifty, he was as lean and fit as Rob's Uncle Nathan. Rob supposed the doctor would never wear a powdered wig such as Josiah Foy and others did. Dr. Boylston's graying hair was drawn back and fastened at the nape of his neck as was Rob's.

Dr. Boylston paused a moment at the door as though to size up the situation. Rachel was still sniffling, and the wounded kitten in Rob's arms gave a faint mew. "Well, well, well. What have we here?" he asked, his voice always gentle. "Has there been an accident?"

"It's not what you'd call an accident exactly," Rob said.

"Mean old Thomas hurt my Kitty," Rachel added.

Dr. Boylston's quiet brown eyes looked at Rob in question. "She's right, sir. Thomas purposely hurt her kitten. He sicced a larger cat after it."

"I see. Bring the patient back here, Robert. Let's have a look." Rob was confident that Dr. Boylston would never make fun of him for having brought in a wounded kitten.

The back of the apothecary shop was Robert's favorite place. Various vials, bowls, bottles, beakers, and mortar and pestles were set about. This was where Dr. Boylston rolled pills, measured tinctures, and mixed salves and ointments. It was on these shelves that he kept his extensive botany collection.

From a shelf the doctor took down a jar of salve. "I'll need your assistance, Robert," he said.

"Yes, sir." Gently Rob drew the quivering kitten from the cradle of his shirt.

"Your mother will not be pleased about that soiled shirt."

Rob looked down at the blood stains on his ruffled silk shirt. "No, sir, I expect not. But it couldn't be helped," he added in defense.

"We'll hope she agrees."

Together they worked to clean the cuts and scratches on the wiggly crying kitten, then apply the salve. It wasn't the first time Rob had worked with Dr. Boylston. In fact, up until only a few months ago, he'd thought he would be allowed to serve his apprenticeship with Dr. Boylston, who was also Rob's good friend. But it wasn't to be.

Dr. Boylston had attempted to convince Josiah Foy to allow Rob to apprentice with him, but Rob's stepfather gave a resounding no. Privately, Josiah told Rob that most doctors were not much better than the paupers begging on the street corners. "Look at my carriage, Robert, then look at Dr. Boylston's carriage."

It was true, Josiah Foy owned one of the nicer, more ornate carriages in all of Boston. It had been specially ordered from England and was drawn by three matched teams of high-stepping dapple-gray horses. But Rob had seen the doctor help people feel better, and that was more important to Rob than a score of fine carriages.

"We're nearly finished now," Dr. Boylston said, glancing over at Rachel. "Kitty will be good as new." Aside to Rob he said, "And you're a fine assistant."

Rob felt his face grow warm. "Thank you, sir."

The doctor took a piece of soft cloth and wrapped it around the kitten who was now calm and purring. "If you hold her in this, Rachel, the ointment won't smear off on your pretty pink dress." Placing the kitten in her arms, he added, "Now let's see what we can do about this stain."

He dipped another cloth in the nearby wooden water bucket and attempted to clean the stains off her dress. "Tell me, young Robert, how are things going at the Foy counting house?"

"Business is as brisk as ever, sir."

"And how about you? How about your work?"

Rob looked down at the silver buckles on his shoes. "I'm trying hard."

"But not too happy, am I correct?"

Rob nodded and said nothing. He wanted to blurt out that he despised every minute in the place, but what good would that do? "Perhaps it will get better with time," the doctor suggested. "Things often do, you know. If you are patient and diligent, the Lord will work it all out. Now let's see if we can do something about your shirt."

With the same gentle touch, Dr. Boylston washed the stains from Rob's shirt. Wanting to change the subject away from the counting house, Rob told Dr. Boylston what Sam had said about the case of smallpox reported aboard the *Seahorse*. "Had you heard about it, sir?"

"I heard. It would seem the captain didn't use wisdom bringing the man ashore as he did." The doctor shook his head as he spoke. "We'd all rest better in our minds if we knew the disease had been kept aboard ship." Dr. Boylston gave the shirt one last rub. "Ah there now, that should satisfy your dear mother."

"Thank you, sir. Rachel, what do you say to Dr. Boylston?"

"Thomas is mean. A mean old bully."

Rob put his arm about Rachel's shoulder and gave it a squeeze. "No, no, Rachel. That's not what I meant. Tell the doctor thank you for his help."

Rachel's tear-streaked face turned up to look at Dr. Boylston. "Thank you for helping Kitty."

"You're welcome young lady. Now mind, you be kind to your brother, both of you. 'Be not overcome with evil, but overcome evil with good.' "

"Yes, sir, we will," Rob promised, but he knew he didn't mean it. It felt good to send Thomas flying into that mud puddle, and he would do it again in a wink.

The three of them walked from the back room across the creaking wooden floor of the shop to the front door. "Scoot on home now. And don't you be worrying about smallpox, young Robert. The selectmen will make an inspection right away. They'll take every precaution and see to it that everything is in order."

"Yes, sir. Thank you again."

As the two of them walked along the roadway, Rob thought about the kindness of Dr. Boylston. A year ago when spring arrived, the doctor had invited Rob to accompany him on a trip to Muddy River. They visited the doctor's boyhood home and together they tramped through the woods and meadows in search of roots and herbs. Rob had fond memories of that trip. He dreamed of it being repeated every spring. Now he was trapped in the horrid old counting house.

"Do you think you'll be in trouble for pushing Thomas into the mud?" Rachel asked, interrupting his thoughts.

"I believe that we'll both be in trouble. We're late for supper, and you know how Father hates for us to be late."

"Freegrace baked pumpkin bread today."

They walked quietly for a time as they mulled over thoughts of Freegrace's savory cooking. Freegrace Symmes had lived with them since Rachel was a baby. No other family wanted to hire the girl since she was badly scarred from a burn. As a little child, Freegrace had fallen into an open fireplace and nearly died. Her face and right arm were deformed from the terrible burns. Rob's mother, however, took pity on her and hired her, and Freegrace never gave her reason to be sorry. She was adept with all the household chores and was a marvel in the kitchen.

"I hope we don't miss the pumpkin bread," Rachel said.

Rob looked down at Rachel's worried little face and felt a pang of remorse. "When we get home, you stay quiet and leave the talking to me."

Rachel nodded.

As they approached the white two-story house on the hill, they both slowed their pace. Rob opened the front gate and let Rachel through first. At the front steps, he attempted to stuff his still-damp shirttail into his breeches, then straightened his tricorn hat. Rachel's lace cap was a bit askew so he reached down to straighten that as well. Kitty was now sleeping peacefully in her arms.

He drew a deep breath and opened the door that led into the foyer. Down the hall they walked, past the great room to the dining room. There Josiah, their mother, Mary, and Thomas were quietly eating supper. Thomas was decked out in a clean suit of clothes with not a speck of mud on him. Freegrace was placing steaming dishes on the mahogany sideboard. Aromas of pumpkin bread filled the air.

"You're late," Josiah said sternly without looking at them. "Supper has already been served. You will go upstairs to your rooms."

Rob straightened himself and stepped forward. "If you please, sir, it was my idea to take the kitten to the apothecary shop. I should be punished and miss my supper, but Rachel did nothing wrong."

Suddenly Rachel was right by his side. "But I wanted to go with Robert to help Kitty get well. Thomas was a bad boy. He hurt my kitten. He should be punished, too."

Now Josiah stopped eating and looked directly at Robert. "It isn't enough that you should hurt your brother, now you're teaching your younger sister to sass her father. Such a poor example for the eldest in the family to set. Letting your anger rule your actions is bad enough. Talking back merely compounds the sin. Go to your rooms, both of you."

Rob could hardly bear the look of sadness on his mother's face. He knew he had disappointed her. However, the smirk on Thomas's face made the anger rise up inside him stronger than before.

In the upstairs hall, as Rachel turned to go into her room, Rob whispered, "Maybe I can figure out a way to get you something to eat later on."

She looked up at him and smiled. "It's all right, Robert, I'm not hungry anyway. Thank you for helping Kitty."

In his room, Rob walked over to the window that looked out past the stables and the cowshed to the Charles River. How unfair everything seemed. How could Thomas get away with such cruelty and he be punished for helping Rachel? If he were apprenticed to Dr. Boylston, he'd ask to live in the room above the apothecary shop. Then he wouldn't have to worry about Thomas any longer. He flopped down on the window seat and cradled his chin in his hands. But if he lived above the shop in Dock Square, who would protect Rachel from Thomas? A sticky question indeed.

Rob turned to gaze at the Queen Anne musket hanging on the wall near his bed. He rose to gently lift it down from the wooden hooks. The musket had been presented to his father, Robert Allerton, Senior, before his father was killed in Queen Anne's War. Rob hadn't even been born when his father died. The weight of the grand musket felt exquisite in his hands. It made him feel as though his father were very close. Rob wondered what his life would have been like had his father lived.

He often asked his mother to tell him more about his soldier father, but she would only say, "The past is past, Robert. Let's dwell on the present and the future."

Just then the door opened and Josiah walked in. Rob quickly replaced the musket on the hooks and sat down at his desk. A lecture was surely coming. Remembering the letter from Josiah's sister, he pulled it from his waistcoat. "A letter from Aunt Esther for you, sir. Mr. Campbell gave it to me this afternoon. I'd nearly forgotten."

"I well understand why you might have forgotten," Josiah said, taking the letter. "The Scripture tells us in Proverbs 16:32 that the man who rules his spirit is better than one who takes a city. Can you tell me what that means?"

Rob studied his stepfather's white powdered and curled wig and his fine ruffled silk waistcoat. He couldn't help but compare him to Dr. Boylston. "It means, sir, that conquest of people and cities is worth nothing if a person cannot control his spirit."

"And did you control your spirit this day?"

Rob clenched his teeth before answering. "No, sir."

"I thought not. Violence is a poor way for a gentleman to settle a difference. If you have a quarrel with your brother you must learn to settle it in gentlemanly fashion as civilized adults. While Thomas may have been in the wrong, your violent reaction was deplorable."

Josiah strode about the room as he spoke, swinging his pearl-handled cane as he did so. "I've spoken with Thomas and he is agreeable to a horse race in the common this coming Saturday. Are you agreeable?"

A horse race. Of course Thomas would choose a horse race. Rob's younger brother was lean and wiry and sat light in the saddle. He was an expert horseman. Rob on the other hand was a bit shorter and more stocky. His horsemanship left much to be desired. He had no desire to race Thomas and lose, but neither would he back down. But then he remembered.

"Excuse me, sir, but I believe I'm to accompany Mother to Punkapaog this Saturday." Once a month Mary visited the Indian prayer town to help in ministry. Appreciative of Rob's help, she always asked him to come along.

"Nonsense," Josiah retorted. "You'll return in plenty of time for an evening race. It certainly won't take long. You're agreeable then?"

"Yes, sir."

Josiah rose and tapped Rob's desk with his cane. "I expect you to prepare a five-page paper on the subject of anger and have it finished before you retire this evening. Bring it to my study when it's completed." He turned to go, then paused. "Make one copy of it in Latin." With that he strode out the door.

Rob groaned as he lifted the lid of his cherrywood desk and drew out sheets of paper. Testing the point of the quill, he dipped it in the ink jar and began to write. How he wished the mere writing about anger would actually remove the anger from his heart.

Later that night, after the paper had been written and delivered to Josiah, a soft tap sounded at his door. It was Freegrace. "Quickly now," she said, "take this and keep mum about it." It was a plate heaped with pumpkin bread slathered in sweet butter. "I'd not do this if the situation were different, but with my own eyes I saw Thomas tormenting Rachel's poor little kitten."

Rob started to speak but she hushed him, so he merely whispered his thanks and quietly closed the door. He listened with satisfaction as her steps proceeded down the hall to Rachel's room.

CHAPTER THREE

The Toy Shop

The next day Rob was fortunate to be sent on several errands that took him out into the glorious sunshine. He left his greatcoat behind, grabbing only his tricorn hat. Long Wharf was a virtual forest of towering ship masts, with so many ships in port at once.

The wharf extended a third of a mile from the shore out into Boston Harbor. Other wharves and shipyards spread out like fingers on either side. Rob was first headed to one of his stepfather's ships, which had docked late the previous afternoon. There were bills of lading and reports to pick up and then deliver back to Josiah's office!

Rollicking strains of a rhythmic sea chantey came from a nearby vessel where the sailors sang as they worked. Running up the gangplank of his stepfather's ship, Rob was met by the pungent aroma of fish. Most all Josiah's ships dealt in the export of mackerel, sturgeon, and cod. While both Noah and Marcus spoke often of their dreams of one day sailing off in a merchant ship, Rob had no such ambitions. To venture down into the captain's quarters, as he was doing now, was as much of a ship as he desired to see.

With the necessary papers in hand, he delivered them back to the counting house. From there, he was sent to the shipyard to deliver a message from Mr. Vetch to the work foreman. Rob was greeted by the banging of hammers and droning of saws. The smell of the freshly cut lumber was much more pleasing to Rob than the stench of fish.

He stopped a moment to survey his stepfather's latest enterprise. The myriad of workers crawled about on the scaffolding like so many ants on a crust of bread. They shouted and called out to one another as they worked.

Rob had no idea how many ships his stepfather owned, nor where they were at any one time. Unfortunately, he would soon find out when he began studying the account books under the watchful eye of Mr. Vetch.

After locating the foreman and delivering the message, Rob lingered along the shoreline for a time, gazing out at the bright, sparkling harbor. Bending down, he selected a few flat stones to see how many times he could make them skip across the waves. The warm spring breeze felt pleasant on his face. How he wished he never had to go back to the counting house.

Presently, the foreman from up on the scaffolding shouted down at him. "Master Robert? Hadn't you better be getting on back?"

Rob threw one last stone and it skipped six times. That was his best. "Yes, sir," he called back and slowly made his way back to Long Wharf.

Noah met him at the front door. "You take longer to run errands than Marcus or I, either one," he said with a sniff. "I wonder why you're even sent. But then I guess we all know why." Rob tried to ignore him and pass on by to learn his next job from Mr. Goddard. "By the way," Noah said, "Mr. Foy wants to see you in his office."

Rob's heart gave a little jump. He hoped he wasn't in trouble again. "What does he want?"

Noah shrugged. "How would I know? He's your father."

"Stepfather," Rob corrected him.

The door to the office was partly ajar. He pulled off his hat, then tapped on the door. "Come in," came Josiah's voice.

"You wanted to see me?"

"Yes, come in." Josiah closed a large leather-bound ledger book and leaned back in his chair. On the wall behind him hung framed paintings of several of his favorite sailing vessels. Nearby on wooden wall hooks hung his smartly tailored scarlet greatcoat trimmed in gold braid and his tricorn hat with its jaunty pheasant feather. As Rob neared the desk, he squinted against the May sunshine streaming in through the tall windows. The warm light lay in neat squares on the wooden floor that he'd scrubbed that very morning.

"Your mother has sent word that you are to go to your Aunt

Elizabeth's toy shop before going home this evening. She has toys ready to be taken out to the village on Saturday."

Rob's sigh of relief was nearly audible. So this is all he wanted? "I'm to go to Aunt Beth's now, sir?"

"Mr. Vetch?" Josiah said to his secretary, "are there any further chores for Master Robert this afternoon?"

Mr. Vetch was standing at his tall desk, which was located in Josiah's office. In the shelves above him were volume after volume of bound books. Mr. Vetch turned to look over his shoulder, peering over his spectacles. "Nothing that cannot wait until tomorrow."

"Very well, then. You have permission to go."

"Yes, sir." Rob moved toward the door, putting his hat on as he went.

"And Robert?"

"Sir?" he said, taking the hat off again.

"Be on time for supper."

"Yes, sir." He reached for the door to push it open.

"And one more thing."

Rob stopped in his tracks. "Yes, sir?"

"If you have any problems with your brother, you will come to me about it first. Is that understood?"

Rob nodded. "Understood, sir." He hurried out before Josiah could think of anything else. Slapping his hat on, he stepped out into the busy street. He knew his stepfather meant well, but it would be impossible to report every little thing Thomas did. He'd just have to handle that matter himself.

Aunt Beth's toy shop was one of Rob's favorite places in Boston—second only to the apothecary shop. Long Wharf led directly to King Street, where shops abounded. He passed the tailor shop, the furniture maker, two alehouses, and the silver-smith before reaching the toy shop. Rob had been told by his mother that when Aunt Beth first opened the toy shop, she and Grandfather Smith and other family members had made all the toys for the shop. Now many of the toys were ordered directly from England.

A little bell tinkled as Rob pushed open the front door. "Hello, Aunt Beth," he called out. "Is that a new rocking horse in the window?"

Then he noticed that his aunt was busy with two customers toward the back of the darkened store. Aunt Beth raised her hand to motion for him to be quiet. He clapped his hand over his mouth and saw her grin. Aunt Beth seemed more like a good friend than his aunt. When Rob was only three, she had cared for him while his mother was employed as a seamstress. Since then, the two had been close friends.

He strolled about the small shop, looking at the toys until the customers left, which seemed to take forever. Uncle Nathan was nowhere to be seen.

As Aunt Beth closed the door, she turned to Rob. "If it isn't the Foy Shipping Line apprentice. Why aren't you at work?"

She stepped over and put her arm around his shoulder. "Is everything all right?"

"Josiah allowed me to leave early to fetch the toys for Mother."

"Ah, you're to pick up Mary's order. I see. But why am I hearing you address your father by his first name? Is that the proper way for a young man to conduct himself?"

Rob turned away and studied a meticulously carved toy ship complete with rigging. He knew this toy had been created by Grandfather Smith's loving hands. "Josiah's not really my father, Aunt Beth."

"You've sat at that man's dinner table for eight years. It appears to me he's had plenty of time to prove himself as a fit father."

Her words gave Rob a pang of guilt. He knew he should be thankful for the wealth in the Foy home. His mother had been rather poor before Josiah had asked her to marry him.

He turned back to his aunt. "I'm sorry. I am thankful to Josiah. I mean, to Father. Aunt Beth, would you tell me some things about my real father? Whenever I ask Mother, she says the past is to be forgotten. But I want to know."

"Come with me, Rob, and let's have a cup of tea."

Aunt Beth lifted the heavy damask curtain that separated the back room from the shop and held it for Rob to pass through. She fixed two cups of tea and invited Rob to sit down at the small wooden table where Grandfather usually sat to carve the tops and toy ships. As they sipped tea, she told Rob a few stories about his handsome father, Robert Allerton.

"Once he made journeyman carpenter, he courted your mother just as though he were a rich merchant," she said. "But he wasn't rich by any means. That's one reason why he fought in Queen Anne's War. He knew there would be extra wages for the fighting men."

"And the musket."

"Yes, the musket. Your musket now." She stopped to drink of the dark strong tea. "Where was I? Oh, yes, he signed up to fight as soon as the word was out that the colony would have to send men to fight the French. I remember that day well. Your Uncle Will was the only member of the family who was excited about your father's decision.

"Your father always was quite impetuous. Robert Allerton seemed to act more quickly than he could think. Sometimes it served him well, other times it got him in trouble."

"I act before I think, and it sure gets me into trouble."

"Oh? What trouble might that be?"

Briefly he told about Thomas causing Rachel's cat to be hurt and how he had pushed Thomas into the mud. Telling about it somehow made him feel better.

"I thought you and Thomas were good friends."

"When we were in Latin School together, it was better," Rob explained. "But now he is constantly making mischief of some kind. And I receive the blame." Rob hadn't taken the time to think about it before, but it had only been in recent months that Thomas had turned on him.

"I should hope that in the midst of your thoughts about your father, you're careful to remember that Thomas also grieves for his dead mother. Pushing your brother into a mud puddle isn't exactly blameless, Rob. Two wrongs never make a right."

"No, ma'am. I don't suppose they do." He fingered the teacup thoughtfully. "Now we are to have a horse race in the common come Saturday evening. I'm sure to lose because Thomas sits light in the saddle. I've always been a bit of a wooden block when I ride. It's sure to be a humiliating event."

The bell on the front door rang, and Aunt Beth excused herself to care for the customer. When she returned, Rob asked, "Do you think I have good traits from my father as well?"

"Ah, yes," she said patting his arm. "His gentleness, his compassion. Robert treated your mother like a queen."

Rob pondered this a moment. Suddenly he remembered what Josiah had said. He jumped to his feet. "Excuse me, Aunt Beth, but I must be on my way. I've been warned not to be late for my supper. I went to bed without it last evening. I don't care to repeat that misfortune."

"I can't blame you," she agreed. From the corner near the fireplace she fetched a coarsely woven bag and handed it over to him. "The toys for the Indian children are in here. I can't quite picture my sister going to the village to visit the Indians. Now that she has the resources, it seems she wants to share them with others. A commendable spirit she has."

"I like being with the Indians, too," Rob said. "Dr. Boylston says we can learn much from them."

"Perhaps so. Say," Aunt Beth said, giving Rob a bright smile, "why not ask one of your Indian friends for a few pointers on how to ride faster?"

"What a good idea," he said, hefting the bag up onto his back. "They don't use saddles, and I've no idea how they manage it. But I can surely ask."

The entry of another customer broke into their conversation. "Be gone with you, Robert Junior. And remember what I said about two wrongs."

Being called Robert Junior made Rob smile. It had a nice sound. He'd like to hear it more often. "I'll try to remember, Aunt Beth. Mother thanks you for the toys." He gave the bag a little shake.

"No thanks are needed. She pays us well for them."

Rob hurried home with a new bounce in his step. Aunt Beth's idea gave him a little ray of hope. He'd at least like to give Thomas a hard race.

CHAPTER FOUR

A Day with Neponset

The part Rob liked best about visiting the Indian village was that Mother let him wear plain clothes. "We aren't there to make a dashing show," she would say. "Our simple frocks will do." Rob needed no convincing. It was his joy to leave the lace, ruffles, and ribbons behind.

The next best thing about this trip was that Sam and his mother, Phoebe, often rode along. Being with Sam for a few hours was a special treat for both boys.

The sun was barely peeping over the horizon when Rob heard the nicker of the horses below his window. He leaped out of bed to go look. The dapple-grays were hitched to the carriage and waiting near the back dooryard. Moseley talked gently to them as he walked around adjusting all the harnesses. Moseley was Josiah's hired footman. A likeable old fellow who, in addition to caring for the stables and driving the carriage, often did odd jobs about the house. On occasion, Josiah offered Moseley lodging at the Foy home, but Moseley preferred to remain in his own small cottage near the wharves.

Although Josiah did not approve of Mary's visits to the village, he still allowed them to take the carriage and use the best horses from the stable. Rob often heard Josiah refer to the Indians as "savages." But then, he'd never been to any of the prayer towns. Rob was sure if Josiah ever met Neponset, his father, Patuckson, and the others, he would feel differently. Josiah tolerated their going only because it was what Mary wanted. He forbade Rachel to go, and Thomas didn't care to go. That pleased Rob. He'd just as soon Thomas stayed home.

Glancing in the wall mirror, Rob brushed back his thick, chestnut-colored hair and fastened it at the nape of his neck with a piece of black ribbon. After hurriedly pulling on his plain shirt, waistcoat, and breeches, he grabbed his hat and bounded down the back stairs to where his mother was waiting.

"There you are," she said. Pulling on her fawn-colored cape, she lifted the hood over the lace cap on her head. At her feet lay the bag of toys, along with two large hampers. Rob knew the hampers were packed full of good food. "These are ready to be loaded," she said. "No sense waiting for Moseley to do it."

Moseley had the door of the carriage open and waiting as Rob approached. "Morning, Master Robert," said Moseley. "Lovely day for our journey."

"That it is, Moseley. That it is."

Moseley took the parcels from Rob and lashed them to the top of the carriage. "There's a shine in your face, Master Robert. Is it because you're given a day's leave from the counting house? Or perhaps it's because of spring."

Rob looked up and gave him a wink. "And perhaps it's both."

It was a special privilege to be allowed to have the day off from work. Was that what Noah and Marcus meant when they said Rob got special favors? It was easy to see how the boys might resent him.

"Thank you, Moseley." Mother's clear voice sounded from behind him. She was studying how Moseley had secured the hampers and the bag of toys. "I believe we're ready."

"Are we to fetch the Lankfords?" Moseley wanted to know.

He reached out to help Mother step up into the carriage. Her full skirts made a swishing sound as she pushed her farthingale hoops through the door. "Yes, the Lankfords are coming along. We'll stop at their house and then be on our way."

"Yes, ma'am." Moseley gave Rob a hand up and closed the door.

The high-spirited horses stepped smartly down Salem Street to Hanover and on to the south part of Boston to where Sam lived. The town was just beginning to awaken and stir about. Sam and Phoebe Lankford were waiting outside, along with Sam's older sister, Martha. Sam teasingly called Martha his "spinster sister." While he teased about it, Rob often thought Sam was somewhat ashamed that his older sister had never married.

Their home was simple compared to the tall white house of Josiah Foy's. Sam's father had perished in Queen Anne's War, as had Rob's, but Sam's mother had never remarried. Sam also had received his father's Queen Anne musket, but one winter when they were cold and hungry, the family had sold it to purchase firewood and food. Rob was careful never to bring up the subject because Sam was still saddened over the loss.

Cheery greetings filled the morning air as Mrs. Lankford and Sam climbed aboard. Rob had heard that Sam's mother had been quite ill when he and Sam were young, but she showed no signs of ill health anymore. Mrs. Lankford was a round-faced happy woman with rosy cheeks and an ample frame.

She, too, had prepared a hamper of food to take, and Moseley secured it above with the others. The flowing skirts and full cloaks of two women nearly filled the inside of the carriage. They called out loud goodbyes to Martha as Moseley urged the horses forward.

They'd not gone far when Sam asked, "Have you folks heard the latest news?"

"Whether we have or have not," Mother said with a laugh, "I'm sure you'll not hesitate to supply us with every detail."

"Good news or bad?" Rob wanted to know. It was too perfect a day to have bad news.

"I'm afraid it's bad," Sam said. "Just as I was leaving the *News Letter* last evening, word came that there are more cases of smallpox aboard the *Seahorse*."

"More?" Mother said, leaning forward, her face suddenly grim. "More than the one? How many more?"

"Eight," Sam answered. "The selectmen of the city discovered them just yesterday. Few people know."

Rob felt as though a rock had settled in his stomach. Eight cases. So many. Would the dread disease come into the city of Boston?

"Governor Shute," Sam went on, "has commissioned the free blacks to begin cleaning the streets as a precaution."

"But will that truly help stop the disease?" Mother asked. There was a catch in her voice.

"They can only hope."

Mrs. Lankford reached over to pat her friend's hand. "There, there, Mary. No need to fear. Our lives are in God's hands. He alone can stay the death angel."

"That's true, Phoebe. How silly of me to let fear take hold." Mary drew out her silk-and-ivory fan and fanned her flushed face. "The stories I've heard since a mere babe are so terrifying. We'll ask the Reverend Checkley to pray with us today for the protection of all our city."

Rob wondered if Dr. Boylston knew about this latest development. Soon the entire town would know. Wanting to talk about more cheerful things, he asked, "Where is the reverend? Isn't he supposed to be going with us?"

"He's to meet us at the Neck," Sam said. "His horse is a light-footed one. He'll be along shortly."

The narrow stretch of land south of Boston called the Neck was the only thoroughfare going in or out of the city. During the month of April, rains flooded the Neck, preventing any such trips. Moseley stopped the carriage for Sam and Rob to jump out and open the gate that led from Boston proper into the Neck. The road leading through the narrowest part was still muddy but passable.

As the boys returned to the carriage, the Reverend Checkley

came galloping up on his large frisky bay. He dismounted at the carriage door to greet Mother and Mrs. Lankford. Addressing the boys, he asked, "Are you ready for a busy day?"

"We're ready," Rob answered. How he wished he were astride his horse, Abrecan, rather than inside the stuffy carriage. But his mother said she preferred he ride along with her.

As they rode along, Mrs. Lankford delighted them with stories. Her own father had been a friend of the missionary John Eliot, who first devised the plan of praying towns for the Indians. Although Rob and Sam had heard the stories numerous times, they never grew weary of hearing how John Eliot ministered among the Indians most of his life, in spite of dangers and opposition.

"After John Eliot spent years translating the Bible into the Algonquian language, many of those Bibles were destroyed during King Philip's War," Mrs. Lankford said as they bumped along. She made the scenes so real Rob could actually see the Indians from the villages being forced into a winter exile to Deer Island during that war. He would have liked to have known the gentle John Eliot who spent so many years among the Indians, helping them to understand the message of the Gospel.

The town of Punkapaog was several miles away from Boston, and by the time they arrived, a few gray clouds had scudded in and threatened of rain. Neponset came riding out on his horse to meet the carriage. Rob stuck his head out the window and waved to his friend. Moseley drew the carriage to a halt in front of the meeting house. The village itself was a hodgepodge of wigwams and rough-hewn log cabins. As usual, many of the Indians ran out to greet them. Unlike in John Eliot's day, nearly all the Indians in Punkapaog now spoke at least some English.

Sam and Rob leaped down out of the carriage just as Neponset rode up and dismounted. "Welcome to you, Robert. And to you, Samuel," he said.

"Hello, Neponset," Rob said, shaking his friend's hand.

"Many moons have passed since you last came to our village. You have been missed."

"The rains," Rob told him, pointing at the sky. "The carriage would have sunk axle-deep in the mud."

Neponset smiled. "I have no such difficulty with my horse."

Rob stepped a little closer and in a lowered voice said, "When we have a moment, I want to ask you something about your horse."

Before he could explain, up walked Neponset's father, Patuckson. The tall, dignified Indian man served as the schoolmaster and leader in the village. He was respected by those in Punkapaog as well as by the Christian Indians in other villages.

Moseley had helped Mother and Mrs. Lankford out of the coach and was bringing down the parcels from atop the carriage.

"We've brought a few gifts for the children," Mother explained after formal greetings with Patuckson. "Can they be gathered to the meeting house early, prior to the meeting hour? We have food as well."

"It can be done." Patuckson turned to the three boys. "Move quickly through the village and gather together all the children," he instructed.

As they moved down the street, Neponset held the reins of his horse, who loped along behind them. It was Rob's chance. "Neponset, I have an important horse race coming up, but I'm nowhere near as fine a horseman as you are. . ."

"Horse race?" Sam interrupted. "You didn't tell me about any

38

horse race. Who are you racing? And where? And when?"

"I couldn't talk about it in front of Mother," Rob said. "It's against Thomas."

"Oh, yes." Sam rolled his eyes. "I think I understand."

"Thomas? This is the brother who is not of your blood. This is right?" Neponset had heard Rob talk about Thomas before.

"That's right. We had a quarrel and my stepfather feels it's only fair to settle with a race. But Thomas is sure to win because he's much lighter than I am."

"Light or heavy makes no difference."

"It doesn't?" Rob had always thought Thomas was better because he was built so wiry.

Just then two or three children came running their way. Neponset stopped to send them on to the meeting house. After the boys had made the rounds through the small village, they stopped in a clearing some distance from the houses.

"White men," Neponset explained, "do not feel the horse."

"Feel the horse? Oh, because of the saddle?"

Neponset nodded. "White man rides with feet. Indian rides with legs. It is so."

He bounded up on the horse, which had only a thin blanket across his back. Rob observed closely as Neponset demonstrated how he guided the horse with the insides of his legs. At one point, he released the bridle strap and still remained in control.

Rob marveled. "May I try?"

Neponset slid to the ground, his leather moccasins raising a puff of dust as he landed. "You may." He reached out to give Rob a leg up.

At first it was awkward, but as he rode for a time, Rob understood what the Indian boy meant. However, it wasn't a skill he would perfect in one day—and the race was to be that evening. "In race," Neponset instructed him, "lie forward, hold mane in fist."

"Like this?" Rob urged the horse into a gentle gallop and practiced leaning forward, drawing his knees up as well.

"Quick to learn," Neponset called out.

Rob turned the horse around and came back to where Sam and Neponset were waiting. "What a difference that would make in the speed of my ride. I don't know of anyone in Boston who rides like this."

"We'd best get back to the meeting house," Sam said, "or we'll be in deep trouble."

Sam was right. As they walked back toward the meeting house, Neponset knocked on a few doors to see if anyone had failed to hear of the visitors' arrival, but the houses were empty. When they arrived back at the center of town, a crowd had gathered about the carriage.

"Boys, there you are," Mrs. Lankford said. "Did you get lost? We need your help handing out the toys."

Rob enjoyed seeing the excited expressions on the faces of the younger children as they received brightly painted tops, toy boats, and dolls for the little girls. Later, lunch was spread on a split-log table in the shade of the trees behind the meeting house. There was a good mixture of New England and Indian food. Rob wanted to go back for a second helping, but his mother gave him a stern look that told him that they were guests and the food was for the villagers.

After lunch, everyone gathered inside the meeting house, and the Reverend Checkley preached a message. There were none of the comforts here that Rob and his family enjoyed at North

Church in Boston. North Church had warm fireplaces, bright whale oil lamps, and three tiers of balconies. This building was quite plain, and there were no backs on the wooden benches.

The Reverend Checkley chose as his text the story of the unforgiving servant in Matthew 18. Rob squirmed on the hard bench as he thought of how he needed to truly forgive Thomas. If only it could be as easy as the reverend made it sound.

In less than a year, Thomas would also be an apprentice in the counting house. Rob could barely imagine what it would be like to be shut up with Thomas all day, every day.

By late afternoon they were in the carriage calling out good-byes to those of the village. Rob mouthed a "thank you" to Neponset as he waved. He wondered if he dared try to ride Abrecan bareback in the race that evening. However, by the time the carriage crossed over the Neck back into Boston, a steady rain was falling. Josiah would never let them race the horses in the rain. Now Rob would have time to practice his technique!

Chapter Five

Can Smallpox Be Stopped?

One morning, two weeks after the trip to the praying town, Rob was on his hands and knees scrubbing the front stone steps of the counting house. While he wasn't fond of scrubbing, this job at least let him enjoy the fresh air of early morning. Presently, Noah and Marcus arrived for work. As they bounded up the steps, Noah's foot made contact with the oak bucket full of water.

Before Rob could jump out of the way, water splashed all over him. He stood to his feet, dripping wet, fuming with anger.

"Goodness, Marcus," Noah said with a cool manner. "Would you look at that. I daresay I'm a bit clumsy this early in the morning." He glanced over at Rob with a wry smile. "I do sincerely apologize, young Robert," he cooed. "I wouldn't want to interfere with your scullery chores."

"That was no accident!" Rob said, stepping up to the taller boy.

"My, my, such accusations. Do calm down." Noah turned away. "Come on, Marcus, let's not dillydally out here. The air seems a bit stuffy."

In a split second Rob had jumped full force on Noah's back, pulling him swiftly to the ground. Taken completely by surprise, Noah had no defense against the onslaught. Once on the ground, they rolled and tumbled, with Rob getting in two good licks, one of which brought a stream of blood from Noah's lip. With one more roll, Rob was able to get on top, pinning Noah to the boards of Long Wharf.

At that moment, the clatter of a carriage could be heard and a voice said, "Robert Allerton, what is the meaning of all this tomfoolery?" It was Josiah, arriving for his day's work in his carriage.

Both boys were on their feet in an instant. "I didn't do a thing, sir," Noah said, swiping at dripping blood with the back of his hand. "I accidentally stumbled over his water bucket, got him a little wet, and he shot off like a loaded cutlass. Never saw anything like it."

Moseley opened the carriage door, and Josiah stepped down, tapping the ground lightly with his pearl-handled cane. "I see. Is that what happened, Marcus?"

Rob glanced at Marcus, but Marcus looked away. "Yes, sir," he said. "Only an accident." Marcus's voice was soft.

"I see." The cane tapped again. "Moseley, take the carriage back to the house."

"Yes, sir."

As the carriage turned about on the wide wharf and clattered away, Josiah said, "Finish your work out here, Robert, and then come to my office."

"Yes, sir."

To the others he said, "Let's not stand about all day. There's work to be done."

As they went in, Noah turned about and made a face at Rob. But his lip was still bleeding.

Later in Josiah's office, Rob stood nervously in front of the cluttered desk.

"Are you aware, young man, that there is a smallpox scare on these wharves?"

Of course he was aware. There'd been talk of little else for the past few weeks. A few more cases were reported each day. "Yes, sir, I'm aware."

"Are you not aware that I have a great deal on my mind right now? I haven't time to keep an eye on you every minute to see that you aren't in another silly scuffle."

Rob wasn't sure what he was supposed to say, so he kept silent.

"Out of respect to your mother, I've not resorted to severe punishment for you. However, if you do not learn to control your temper, severe punishment is precisely what will come to you."

"Yes, sir." Rob wondered what severe punishment consisted of, but he feared to ask.

"After supper this evening, report to my study, and I'll assign another paper for you to write. Meanwhile, there's too much work to be done in this counting house for you to spend time fighting about petty differences. Do I make myself clear?"

"Very clear, sir." Rob didn't mind writing another paper. However, he'd been spending every evening he could riding Abrecan and practicing the technique he'd learned from Neponset. His progress was coming along beautifully.

"Mr. Vetch?" Josiah addressed his secretary. "Do you have errands for Robert? Perhaps he can run off some of his excessive energy."

"There are errands to run," said Mr. Vetch as he approached the desk. He handed Rob a rolled paper. "Another ad for the *News Letter*. And also a parcel to deliver. Come with me, Master Robert."

As they went out the door, Josiah called after him. "Don't forget what I said."

"I won't forget."

In the warehouse located next to the counting house, Mr. Vetch handed Rob a small wooden box. "For Dr. Boylston. It says 'fragile' on it. Must be some of his strange little bottles from London."

"For Dr. Boylston?" Rob's face brightened. A trip to the apothecary shop would certainly redeem this day in perfect order.

"You like that shop, Master Robert?" Mr. Vetch peered at him over his spectacles.

Rob nodded. No one would ever know how much he loved it.

"If you like it so much, why are you not apprenticed there?"

Rob looked up at the kindly old man. How had he guessed? "I'm here because of Josiah's orders. He feels my financial opportunities are greater here."

"So that's it. But the money doesn't matter to you?"

"Oh, not at all. I'd just as soon live over by the Lankfords in a plain old house and wear leather breeches."

Mr. Vetch covered his mouth, but the smile wasn't hidden. "Tell me," he said after a moment. "Have you prayed about this matter?"

"Prayed?"

"Yes. Have you told God about your longing?"

"No, sir." Rob didn't see how God would have much say-so in this matter.

"Might I suggest you give it a try?"

Rob mulled it over and felt it might be a good idea. It was certainly a new thought. "I'll do it, sir. And thank you."

"Now get on with you. You have work to do."

Rob's feet barely touched the ground as he ran to Dock Square. Halfway there, he suddenly remembered he was carrying glass, which slowed him down to a fast walk. As he approached Dr. Boylston's shop, he spied a two-wheeled hooded carriage parked just outside. Rob recognized it as belonging to the Reverend Cotton Mather.

As Rob entered the darkened shop, it took a moment for his eyes to adjust. The two men were in the back room talking. Dr. Boylston came to the doorway. "Ah, Robert. Good to see you. What brings you this way?"

"A package for you, Dr. Boylston."

The reverend also stepped into the shop from the back. His long powdered wig gave him a solemn appearance. Rob had always admired this learned man who often came to their home for visits. "Greetings, lad. You're looking fit."

"Thank you, Reverend."

"If you have a moment, please wait," Dr. Boylston told Rob. "We're nearly finished."

How could Robert not have a moment for his friend? "I'll wait."

"You were saying about the inoculation?" Dr. Boylston said to the minister.

"I've read reports about this operation given to me by Dr. Douglass." The Reverend Mather leaned on his stout cane as he spoke. "But I learned about it firsthand from my slave, Onesimus."

Rob stepped over to the shelves containing the jars with leeches swimming about in pond water. Dr. Boylston often used the leeches to bleed his patients when they were ill. Rob couldn't help but overhear the conversation. What in the world was an inoculation?

"Your slave, Reverend? What would he know about an inoculation?"

"He's had one. That's how he knows. Showed me the scar right on his arm. Onesimus has no fear of the smallpox, I can tell you that."

"I declare," Dr. Boylston said thoughtfully. "An African native, and he knows about this practice. How interesting. How long have you known this?"

"For several years. I've also read reports given to me by Dr. Douglass verifying the success of the operations in Turkey."

"As have I. Do you know what this could mean?"

Rob inched closer in hopes of hearing the answer.

"It could mean, Dr. Boylston, that if we inoculate, there might be a chance of staying the death angel in Boston."

There was excitement in the voice of the minister such as Rob had never heard before. "I believe," said the Reverend Mather, "the first step is to formulate a letter to all Boston physicians suggesting they come together for a consultation on the matter. Do you agree?"

"Quite. Shall I help in that?"

"Oh no, doctor. You have enough to do. I'll see to it that the letter is done quickly. I must be going now. Good day, Doctor. Good day, young Robert."

As soon as the pastor was out the door, Rob hurried to Dr. Boylston's side. "What is an inoculation, and how can it stop the smallpox?"

"There you go with that curious mind of yours. I thought you had a package for me. Aren't you going to deliver it?"

Rob had almost forgotten why he was there. He'd left the package lying on the shelf. Running to fetch it, he said, "It's here, sir. Forgive me."

Dr. Boylston laughed. It was a friendly laugh that always made Rob know everything was all right. "Thank you for your efficient delivery service." He made a funny little bow, then unwrapped the box and lifted out slender glass containers packed in fluffy cork sawdust. "These will be very useful if we proceed with the inoculations."

"But please, sir, you've still not told me. What is an inoculation?"

Dr. Boylston gathered the parcel and the glass containers and headed toward the back room. Rob followed on his heels. "An inoculation means we give a person a little case of smallpox which renders that person immune from a big case of smallpox."

"But that's amazing! How is it done?"

"It's quite simple, actually. A little pus is taken from a sore of an infected person. It is then administered into a tiny cut or opening on the body of a well person. The well person may have a few sores break out on his body, but in a few days it is over and he is well again."

The doctor set the glass containers on a shelf inside a cupboard. "The best part is that the person then becomes immune for the rest of his life."

Rob was delighted with this concept. He'd never heard anything like it. If this was true, then everyone in Boston should be inoculated. He couldn't wait to tell his family so they all could receive this miraculous protection.

"Does the person who is inoculated get sick at all?" Rob wanted to know.

"Different people will, no doubt, react differently. Remember, Robert, this practice is rather new to me. I'll be working in new territory, like an experiment. There is always an element of risk."

"But the risk would be worth it, is that right?"

Dr. Boylston seated himself in a Windsor chair near his desk and looked up at Rob. "In my mind it is, but that's no guarantee others will agree."

Rob couldn't imagine anyone disagreeing. It seemed so clear. So simple. So wonderful.

"Are you due back at the counting house?"

"What? No, I still must make a delivery to the *News Letter*." Rob was so caught up in all this new thinking that he'd almost forgotten. "I'd better hurry along. Good day, sir. I truly wish I were working here so I could assist you in this work."

Dr. Boylston nodded. "So do I, Robert. So do I."

At the *News Letter* office, Sam was busy helping Mr. Campbell operate the large printing press at the back of the shop. Rob placed the advertisement from Josiah on Mr. Campbell's desk and went back to watch.

Sam placed a sheet of clean paper on the tympan, then quickly moved his fingers out of the way as Mr. Campbell rolled the carriage in and out to print on the page. Sam peeled off the freshly printed page and laid it aside to dry, hurriedly grabbing yet another clean sheet to begin the process all over again.

Greetings were exchanged over the clatter of the press, after which Rob said, "Have you heard the news?" That was Sam's favorite phrase, and it was a novelty to be able to say it first.

"I've heard that the smallpox scare is growing," said Mr. Campbell. "And that people are leaving town."

Leaving town? Now that was news. Rob hadn't realized people would simply leave. "This has to do with smallpox, but it's good news. The doctors can use something called inoculation that will stop it."

Mr. Campbell held back the carriage for a moment. "Who have you been talking to?"

"Dr. Boylston and the Reverend Mather. The reverend is planning to call a meeting of all the doctors of Boston to set up a plan."

Sam quickly caught the momentum of Rob's excitement. "What a turn of events that would be. That's great news!"

Mr. Campbell picked up the leather ink bag and inked the type afresh. "It'll never happen, mark my words."

Rob suddenly felt deflated. "Never? But why?"

"Not that I wouldn't want it to happen, mind you." He shook his head. "Ah don't mind me, Robert. I may be getting cynical in my greater years. Time can do that to a person. I've seen too much." He pushed the carriage over the clean paper with a clatter and bang and pulled it back again. "I'm pleased to hear the Reverend Cotton Mather is taking a stand in the matter. I'll be sure to let him know I'll help however I can."

"He'll be pleased to learn that, sir. I must be going now."

"The next time you come," Sam said, "perhaps we won't be so busy. Then you can explain all about inoculations."

"I will, I will," he said as he left. "The advertisement is on your desk, Mr. Campbell." And with that he was out the door.

That evening at the Foy dinner table, Josiah began to talk about Mother and Rachel going to his sister's home in Roxbury. "Esther requested in her letter of a few weeks ago that you and Rachel come for a spell. This appears to be the most opportune time, Mary."

"But I can't leave," Rob's mother said. "There's no doctor to help at the village. Phoebe and I will be needed there, perhaps even more than in previous days."

Josiah was never one to push his wife, and he seemed to always respect her wishes. Today was no different. "It grieves me deeply that you would put yourself and Rachel in peril, my dear. Perhaps in a week or two you will feel differently."

"Perhaps. But no matter what happens, I know the Lord will watch over us."

Rob could remain quiet no longer. "You can give the Lord a helping hand with an inoculation," he said. "All of us can be inoculated and be saved from the spread of smallpox."

All eyes around their polished mahogany table were upon him.

"Whatever are you talking about, Robert?" his mother asked. "What is this inoculation? What does it mean?"

"I've heard of it," Josiah said. "It's a pagan custom wherein a person cuts his own skin to attain the disease on purpose. It's a ghastly thought. An ungodly practice to be sure."

Josiah's words were startling. His description sounded nothing like what Dr. Boylston and the Reverend Mather had discussed.

"And how would you know anything about such matters?" Thomas butted in. "Who would tell you about a pagan ritual?"

"But it's not a pagan ritual. It's an operation. Dr. Boylston said so."

"Ah, I thought as much," Josiah said. "Dr. Boylston, the back-woodsman who calls himself a doctor."

"He is a doctor!" Rob said, raising his voice in defense of his friend.

"Robert, please," Mother cautioned.

"Mother, you know Dr. Boylston is a good doctor. He's studied with both his father and with Dr. Cutler. He's performed successful surgeries, and he knows this experiment can work."

"There, you said the word." Josiah slammed his knife to the table. "Experiment. I am expected to allow this unlearned man to experiment on my family? Never! You're too young to have seen anyone die with smallpox, Robert. For a person to purposely inflict his body with this wretched disease is insane. I forbid it to be spoken of in my home."

Silence hung heavy as Freegrace came into the room to take their plates and to serve sweet cakes and raisin pudding. It was Rob's favorite dessert, but his appetite had fled.

Presently Josiah spoke again. "If this crazed man proceeds with this experiment on human lives and if someone should die, I pray to God the magistrates will try him for manslaughter."

Manslaughter? Rob could scarcely believe what he was hearing. There was nothing more he could say, but now he knew full well what Mr. Campbell meant. Convincing people about the inoculations would not be easy.

CHAPTER SIX

Trapped in the Counting House

Rob awoke with a start, then wondered what had awakened him. He lay in his curtained bed, straining to listen. Mother and Freegrace had finished with the spring cleaning last week, so the heavy bed curtains had been taken down and the lightweight ones put in their place. Through the hanging cloth, he could see moonlight spilling in through his window. Perhaps he'd heard an animal outside his open window.

He rose and stepped down from the tall bed using the step stool at his bedside. There! He paused as he heard it again—a whining, whimpering sound. At the window he peered down into the dooryard but saw nothing. When the sound came again, it seemed farther away.

Stepping across the room to his doorway, he listened again. It was coming from down the hall—from Rachel's room. The whimpering was Rachel. With his nightshirt billowing, Rob hurried down to her room and slipped inside.

"Rachel? Rachel, what's the matter? Why are you crying?"

"Don't hurt me, Robert," he heard her tiny voice answer.

He drew back the gauzy material to see Rachel looking at him with eyes wide with fear. "Rachel, are you dreaming? It's me, Robert."

Gently he sat down on the edge of her bed, and she drew back. This wasn't like Rachel at all. "Don't hurt me, please!" she said with a whimper.

"I could never hurt you, little sister. How could I hurt you?"

"Thomas said you will kill us all. Please don't kill me." Her tiny body was trembling.

Rob felt a sick feeling sweep over him. What had Thomas done now? "Rachel, try to calm down. What did Thomas say?"

A little sob caught in her throat. "He said you want to 'noculate me and kill me. Do you, Rob?"

Rob rubbed his hands over his eyes and gritted his teeth against the anger that was building. He'd like to run into Thomas's room and thrash the boy soundly for this hateful deed.

"Come here, Rachel. Let's go over to the window where it's light and talk. See, the moon is bright."

At first she hesitated, but then she took his outstretched hand. He lifted her down from the bed and helped her climb up onto the window seat. Meanwhile, Rob was struggling to swallow his rage.

"Which drawer holds your handkerchiefs?" he asked.

"Top middle."

He brought her a lacy handkerchief and wiped her eyes and let her blow her nose. "Now, Rachel, I want you to think back to the day we took Kitty to the apothecary shop. Remember?"

She nodded and made a little hiccup.

"Remember how kind Dr. Boylston was to us?"

Again she nodded. "Thomas was mean."

"Let's don't talk about Thomas right now," Rob suggested. "Let's talk about Dr. Boylston. He knows how to help people. He doesn't want to hurt anyone. An inoculation makes a person just a little bit sick and keeps them from getting bad, bad sick. Understand?"

"Are you going to 'noculate me?" she asked, eyes still wide.

Rob sighed. "Rachel, I wouldn't know how to do an inoculation. I'm not a doctor. I wish I were, but I'm not."

"You don't know how?"

"I don't know how."

Insect noises floated in on the June night. In the distance dogs barked, and a night watch called out, "Three o'clock and all's well. Three o'clock and all's well."

After a moment, Rachel said, "You can't 'noculate me and hurt me?"

Rob took hold of Rachel's small shoulders and said, "Rachel, if I knew how to do the inoculation and if I thought it would save your life, I would do it and do it quickly. But I would never, never harm you. Do you believe me?"

"But Thomas said. . ."

"Forget what Thomas said."

She pouted a moment, then looked up at Rob. "I'll try."

"Now, let's get you back to bed." He took her hand and led her across the soft hooked rug to her bed. "And promise me, whatever Thomas says to you, you'll come and tell me." He lifted her into the bed. "Promise?"

"I promise."

"Good. Now you can stop being afraid and go back to sleep."

"Robert?"

"Yes?"

"I'm glad you're not going to kill me."

Rob gave an involuntary shudder as a brisk breeze blew in through the open window. "I want to be a doctor, Rachel. Doctors save lives."

"How can you be a doctor at the counting house?" she asked.

"That's a good question, Rachel. Mr. Vetch told me to pray about it. Will you help me pray?"

"Mm hm. I'll pray."

"Thank you. Good night, Rachel."

"Good night, Robert."

After that episode, sleep was a long time coming for Rob. It might have been the perfect time to talk to the Lord about the unbearable situation at the counting house. But how could he ask the Lord for help when he was so angry with Thomas?

The next morning, the crowing of the old rooster just below Rob's window roused him into wakefulness. "Thanks be to you, noisy rooster," he said as he jumped out of bed. "I need to be up early today."

From the tall dresser with the brass knobs, he pulled out a fresh outer shirt that had ruffles on the sleeves. He quickly dressed in his nankeen knee breeches and fastened his silk stockings with ribbon garters. His yellow embroidered waistcoat had been laundered by Freegrace only a few days earlier and smelled of fresh outdoors. Jumping into his buckle shoes he hurried downstairs. His neckband, complete with even more ruffles that he despised, he stuffed in the pocket of his waistcoat.

Although Moseley did most of the work in the stables, both Thomas and Rob had assigned chores given them by Josiah. It was Rob's week to carry the water from the well to the water troughs. There was one trough in the stables and another in the shed where the two milk cows were kept. Freegrace and Mother tended to the milking and the dairy, for which Rob was thankful.

Freegrace was in the dooryard searching among the bushes for eggs that the hens or the geese might have laid. Her basket was half full. Later she and Thomas would set about weeding the kitchen garden.

"Good morning, Freegrace."

"Say there, Master Robert. You're up early."

"Yes, ma'am." He hurried on to the well, not wanting to stop for a visit. Rob wanted to talk to his mother alone, and this was the best time to do so—but he would have to hurry. It took several trips from the well to the stables and shed, toting the heavy, sloshing buckets before the troughs were filled. Finally the job was completed.

He hurried back into the house, but the kitchen was empty. Sounds of his mother's singing in the buttery led him in that direction. The cool lean-to was located just outside the kitchen. Here the shelves were stacked with round cheeses and molds of butter. Churns, butter molds, and wooden bowls were strewn about. Rob breathed deeply of the rich aroma of cheese.

Mother was scrubbing out the churn with a stiff-bristled brush. She looked up as he came through the door. "You're dressed in your fine clothes to do your chores?"

"I was in a hurry."

"You should always do the chores dressed in your plain garments, then change for work. Where's your neckband?"

He patted his pocket. "Here."

"Don't forget to put it on before you get to the counting house. Are the horses watered?" she wanted to know.

"Yes, ma'am."

"And you've eaten?"

"Yes, ma'am."

"Then hadn't you best be on your way?"

"If you please, may I speak my mind a moment?"

Mother laid down the brush and pushed from her face wisps of hair that had fallen from beneath her lace cap. "You can always speak your mind with me, Robert. You know that."

"It's about the smallpox inoculations, Mother. I trust Dr. Boylston completely, and I'm quite confident he would never harm anyone."

"Now, Robert, you heard your father last evening. We're not to bring up the subject again."

"But that's unfair. You just said I could speak my mind." He stepped over, took hold of her arm, and gently led her out into the dooryard. "There now," Rob said. "Josiah said we were forbidden to speak of inoculations in his house, but we are no longer in his house."

"Robert Allerton, you are most surely your father's son. So strong-headed."

Her comment pleased Rob, but he let it pass. "Mother, I'm confident Dr. Boylston is correct in this matter. And even our own preacher believes this operation can be a success. The Reverend Mather's own slave, Onesimus, has a scar to prove that it's a safe procedure."

"What are you asking me, Robert?"

"That you please speak to Josiah about this. He'll listen to you. Persuade him to discuss this with Dr. Boylston. Perhaps he'll then see how important it is to at least inoculate Rachel."

Mother sighed. She pushed strands of hair back under her lace cap. "I'll try, but I can promise you nothing. I'm not so sure I'm convinced yet. I know Dr. Boylston means well, but it's such a frightening thing, smallpox is. It's not child's play, Robert."

"All the more reason to protect ourselves against it."

His mother shook her head. "You are growing to be a man, my son. You have such a mind of your own. Let me think on this and pray. We'll talk about it later. Now off to work with you."

Later, as Robert walked along dusty Salem Street toward Long Wharf, he passed a number of carts traveling in the direction of the Charles River. These were the families who were leaving the city to seek safety in another place. They would take the ferry at the river over to Charlestown. If Rob's mother refused to consider the inoculation, he hoped she would do this very thing. And quite soon!

By the following week, the letter from the Reverend Mather had been distributed to all the physicians in Boston. Sam knew most of the details and even knew what the letter said. At the *News Letter* office one afternoon, he explained it to Rob.

"The letter was polite and informative," Sam said. "Quite simply, it invited the physicians to gather for a consultation about the inoculation operation."

"A good letter it was, too," Mr. Campbell chimed in. "But so far it's been ignored, and more's the pity for it." The two printers were taking afternoon tea when Rob arrived, and the lull in work created a good opportunity for talking.

"Why do you think the other doctors are ignoring him?" Rob asked.

Mr. Campbell offered Rob a tin of crackers and waited until he had taken one before answering. "My first guess is pride."

"Pride? How can that be?"

"Perhaps they don't take kindly to a preacher telling them how to conduct their doctoring business."

"But he's not telling them. . ."

"Now, now." Mr. Campbell put up his hand. "I said 'perhaps.' A body ought not jump to conclusions. Best thing now is to wait and see. It's only been a week since the letter was circulated. A meeting still may occur."

"Well, I can vouch for one thing," Rob said as he finished the hardtack cracker. "Dr. Boylston won't let pride rule him."

Sam raised his cup of tea. "And I believe you're right," he agreed.

"Let's wait and see" was all Mr. Campbell would say.

Mr. Campbell and most people his age had survived a previous smallpox epidemic. While no one knew why this was so, it seemed that children and other people who hadn't lived through an earlier smallpox epidemic were more at risk for getting sick. Every day more oxcarts, carriages, and packhorses made their way either to the Neck or to the Charles River ferry in a mass exodus. Parents wanted to get their children to safety.

Toward the end of June, the mood at the counting house had grown more quiet. Noah stopped playing tricks, and even Mr. Vetch was somber. Josiah spent long hours at his desk and on board the ships that were arriving and departing. Some evenings he didn't come home until long after Rob had gone to bed.

Talk of possible quarantines and closing the harbor forced Josiah to work at a feverish pace. Workers and sailors on the wharf raced to load and unload before such a closing might come to pass. The latest issue of the *News Letter* reported growing numbers of sick in the city.

One morning Rob was called into Josiah's office. "You wanted to see me, sir?" he said as he entered the door. Mr. Vetch didn't even look up from his account books as Rob entered.

"Yes, Robert. Beginning tomorrow morning I want you to spend the morning hours in here with Mr. Vetch. He will set you to copying vouchers and bills of lading."

Something in Rob's midsection gave a little lurch. This was what he'd been dreading. "So soon, sir? What about my other chores?"

"We've no idea how much time we have before the entire harbor may be closed. The ships that are now anchored must be loaded quickly and sent off before that occurs. Every transaction is of the utmost urgency, is that understood?"

"Yes, sir."

"Do the sweeping, fill the ink pots and sand jars, sharpen all the quills, then report here to Mr. Vetch."

"Yes, sir."

So it had finally come. The thing that Rob dreaded most. Now he would be more of a prisoner than ever, perched on a high stool, forced to sit at a desk and meticulously create four copies of all the forms.

That afternoon as he walked home, the glorious June sunshine lit up the countryside. Flower gardens were bursting into glorious reds, blues, and yellows, and the great shade trees were fully leafed out, waving like giant feathers. Summer, he reasoned, should be a time of joy and merriment, but Rob's mood was sulky and glum.

CHAPTER SEVEN

The Race

Back at the house, there were water troughs to fill once again. A load of wood had been delivered during the day, so after the water was carried, Rob took the axe and split kindling. The smaller sticks would suffice as oven wood for tomorrow's baking. Later Moseley showed up, and together they stacked the logs in the woodshed.

Out in the orchard, Rachel played beneath the apple trees with her dolls and Kitty. Rob envied her free playtime. Thomas seemed to be nowhere about.

The kitchen was steamy hot as Rob stepped inside and deposited his armload of kindling in the woodbox next to the fireplace. A hambone simmered in the black kettle suspended over the fire. Freegrace pulled a pan of milk biscuits out of the side oven. The heat from the oven turned the scars on her face and arms a splotchy red.

Mother came in from the dining room. "Supper will be ready soon, Rob. Find your brother and tell him please."

"I've not seen him. He wasn't outside."

"He was given extra work by the schoolmaster today. He's in his room finishing the assignment."

"Extra work? Why?"

Mother gave him a stern look. "That doesn't appear to be of your concern, now does it?"

"No, ma'am, I suppose not."

"Then off with you."

Rob took the main stairs two at a time, swinging around the banister at the landing. Thomas's room was the first one in the second floor hall, but the room was empty. Just then he heard a rustling noise coming from his own room farther down the hallway.

He quieted his steps and tiptoed to his door, which was slightly ajar. Thomas was sitting on Rob's bed, and in his hands he held the Queen Anne musket.

Rob flew across the room. "You dolt!" he yelled. "You dunderhead! Take your hands off my musket!"

"I'm not hurting your old gun!" Thomas was barely able to drop the gun on the bed and leap to his feet before Rob attacked.

Rob felt his fist connect soundly with Thomas's nose. Blood flowed. Another good smack with his left fist and Thomas was lying flat on the braided rug in the middle of the room. Rob leaped in the middle of him with fists flying.

"That's my father's musket, and you're not to touch it!" he cried. "Never, never, never!"

Suddenly his mother was at the doorway shouting at him, bringing him to his senses. "Robert Allerton, you get off your brother this very instant." She dragged him off. Thomas rolled on his side, groaning loudly.

Freegrace must have been on Mother's heels. She helped Thomas to his feet and held her apron to his bleeding nose.

"Let's get you to the kitchen where we can put a cool cloth on that nose," she said. Rob saw her glance about the room till she saw the musket on the bed. A look of knowing came over her. She shook her head as she assisted Thomas out the door.

"Bully!" Thomas shouted over his shoulder as he stumbled along beside Freegrace. "Nothing but a bully."

Now the pain in Rob's knuckles came alive. Still sitting on the floor, he rubbed first one and then the other, gazing at the redness, not wanting to look in Mother's eyes. Again, he had disappointed her.

"Pray tell what terrible act did your brother commit to unleash such fury from you?" Mother had seated herself at his desk chair.

Rob pointed to the bed.

"You can talk. Or do your fists always speak for you?"

Rob's voice sounded small and squeaky. "He took down the

musket—Father's musket."

"I see. From this distance, I would say the musket of which you speak is still in one piece. I don't believe Thomas harmed it any."

Rob had no words. He felt very small, sitting there at his mother's feet.

"I know the musket is important to you, but if it causes you to harm another person, then you've placed a wrong value upon it."

"Yes, ma'am." Robert couldn't fully understand, but something deep inside him didn't want Thomas to ever touch his father's special musket.

"Moseley tells me that Josiah will be home for our evening meal. I shall have to tell him what happened."

"Yes, ma'am."

She stood to go. "How I pray that you might learn to think before you act."

He dared a quick look at her sad eyes. He loved her very much, and it was never his intention to cause her distress.

Later at supper, Josiah was filled in on the frightful details of the fight. Mother also told him how Thomas had made trouble at Latin School that day. But Thomas's mischief seemed minor compared to the split lip and bloody nose Rob had caused.

"I believe we're past due for the horse race at the common," Josiah said. "Fistfighting is something that is done by South Ender ragamuffins. The two of you are to conduct yourselves as gentlemen."

Rob resented Josiah's remark about South Enders since that was where Sam lived, but now was not the time to discuss it. Shortly after the supper hour was over, the boys were astride their saddled mounts loping silently behind Josiah's carriage.

The race made little sense to Rob. No matter what happened,

it would never change how he felt about that musket.

When they arrived at the common, Moseley drew the carriage to a halt, and Josiah stepped down, adjusting his hat with the colorful pheasant feather.

A few cows peacefully grazed the plentiful summer grass of the common, waiting for their owners to come take them home. Usually there were ladies strolling about, but the smallpox scare had changed all that.

"See the hemlock tree there by the fence?" Josiah was saying. "The second one from the gate that leads to Beacon Street?"

"Yes, sir," answered Thomas eagerly. His horse, Dapper, switched his tail impatiently. Both appeared ready to fly across the grassy acres of Boston Common.

"You will ride to that hemlock tree and back here to the carriage. Begin when I shout, 'Go.'"

"I need just a moment, sir." Rob slid out of the saddle before Josiah could protest. No rules had been mentioned about saddles. Quickly he uncinched the girth and pulled off the saddle, slinging it to the ground at the rear of the carriage.

"What's the meaning of this?" Josiah asked.

"I'm riding bareback."

"Suit yourself, but don't look to anyone here for help when you land in the dirt."

Rob let the reins fall slack, grabbed a handful of Abrecan's mane, and hiked up. "I'm not planning to fall, sir."

In the days since he'd been riding alone without the saddle, the gelding had come to love the freedom from the binding leather. Now Abrecan, too, displayed a readiness. Rob glanced at Thomas and marveled that the cockiness was gone. His stepbrother appeared to be a little worried.

At Josiah's shout, the boys released the horses in a dead run. By the time they reached the hemlock tree, Thomas was a hairsbreadth ahead. Rob suddenly realized he'd not practiced sharp turns, and as he pulled the reins for Abrecan to turn, he very nearly slid off. Taking a moment to right himself gave Thomas a clear lead.

In spite of his error, Rob sensed the possibility of winning. He lay nearly prone and squeezed with his knees, letting Abrecan fly. Thomas whipped Dapper in a desperate attempt to stay ahead. Midway between the hemlock tree and the carriage, Abrecan sailed past as though Dapper were standing still. Rob couldn't remember a more exhilarating sensation. Abrecan was beyond the carriage before Rob could manage to get him slowed down.

"Unfair!" Thomas shouted as he drew Dapper up at the finish. "That was an unfair race."

"How do you find it unfair?" Josiah asked.

"Make him saddle up and then race."

"No rules were stated about having a saddle," Rob said as he trotted up.

"That's true." Josiah pulled off his hat and dabbed at his forehead with a silk handkerchief. He glanced up at Moseley, who was still perched in the driver's seat, holding the reins of the team. Moseley gave a slight shrug and said nothing.

"Let's make it two out of three," Thomas demanded.

"In this heat?" Rob put in. "That's too hard on the horses. I won fairly, and it's done. Let's go home." Without wanting to discuss it further, he jumped off and grabbed up his saddle. "May I place this in the carriage, sir? I'd just as soon not put it back on."

Josiah gave a sigh and replaced his hat. Moseley jumped

down and opened the carriage door. Josiah took the saddle, heaved it on the floor of the carriage, and stepped in after it.

With that done, Rob turned Abrecan and headed out for home. Although the speed had been terribly exciting, winning the race didn't make him feel any better. In fact, the look of dejection on Thomas's face made him feel rather sad.

June was barely half over when Mother announced she would be making another trip to Punkapaog. Her announcement came on another evening when Josiah happened to be home for supper. He quickly protested.

"It's been only a short time since you were there, Mary. There's no need for you to go again so soon. Especially now with the threat of smallpox everywhere. It may have broken out in the village already."

"But don't you see," Rob's mother said in her quiet voice, "that's exactly why we must go. There's no doctor there, and someone needs to know how they're faring."

"Why must it be you?" he said.

"Why God compels us to follow His leading, I cannot explain," she said.

The news cheered Rob. Going to the village would get him out of Boston and out of the counting house, if only for a few hours.

The Saturday of their journey was the warmest day of the summer so far. Inside the carriage the air was stuffy. Sam, however, was his usual jovial self. Rob marveled that nothing seemed to affect his redheaded friend. When Sam talked about the news from the paper, he spoke of it all the same whether the news was good or bad.

"Have you heard about the Harvard commencement?" he

asked. Of course Mrs. Lankford had heard, since Sam spilled all the news to her first thing every evening. But she remained silent.

"There's nothing new about Harvard's commencement," Rob quipped. "It's held every June."

"Yes, but this year it's being held privately. Only the parents and families of the graduates are allowed in."

"But why?" Rob wanted to know. Most of Josiah's friends were Harvard graduates, and they always traveled to Charlestown for the commencement ceremonies.

"Because of the smallpox epidemic," Sam said.

"But it's not an epidemic," Rob protested. He hated the sound of the word. "There's only been a few cases so far."

"Mr. Campbell says the selectmen and magistrates aren't revealing the true number so as to prevent panic."

"From the looks of the cartloads of people who are leaving," Mrs. Lankford put in, "I'd say mild panic has already begun."

When they arrived at the praying town, it was as Mother had feared. There were already two cases of the dread disease. Mother, Mrs. Lankford, and the Reverend Checkley instructed the Indians in the best methods to care for the sick.

Neponset seemed pleased to see Rob and Sam. "Please tell if you won the horse race," he said to Rob. "No saddle is better, do you agree?"

They were sitting on the ground in the warm sun near the edge of a cornfield. The waist-high stalks were glossy green, a promise of a good harvest to come.

Rob laughed at Neponset's comment. "I certainly agree about no saddle. At first, the race was put off because of rain and my father's business, but when it finally came, I won."

"Good. Very good." Neponset nodded gravely.

"Well, I've never seen this Indian-style riding," Sam said. "Let's have a little demonstration."

"Do you mind, Neponset? May I borrow your horse?"

Neponset smiled. "I, too, want to see you ride as the Indian rides." He untied the horse, which was tethered to a nearby tree, and handed the lead rope to Rob. He then reached out to give Rob a hand up, but Rob shook his head.

"Watch this." Rob grabbed the mane and rope, and with a mighty leap and strong swing, he was up and on. Sam laughed and clapped. Rob rode far enough to show both of them how well he had mastered the art of bareback riding.

By the time he dismounted, Sam was all agog. "You're magnificent, Rob. Next November at the election day celebration, we'll enter you in all the races. You can win a few shillings."

"I don't think I'm quite that fast," Rob said, but it was good to have Sam making all the fuss.

"Almost as good as me," Neponset said with a smile.

Just then Mrs. Lankford called them from the door of the meeting house. "Come, boys. The meeting's about to begin."

"We're coming," Sam called back.

"Neponset," Rob said, turning to his friend, "thank you for teaching me. I appreciate it more than I can say." He reached into the pocket of his breeches and pulled out his small jackknife. "I want you to have this." The gesture wasn't something Rob had planned, but it seemed right.

Neponset's hand closed over Rob's as he took the knife. "This is a good gift. I shall treasure it always. I, too, have a gift for each of you. Wait here." He ran to his cabin near the meeting house and quickly returned. Into each boy's hand he placed a large white tooth.

"Taken from the mighty black bear killed by the father of my father. We carry to frighten evil spirits." Pointing skyward he added, "The Good Spirit now dwells with me. Fear of death and bad spirits has fled. Take them as a token of our friendship."

Rob felt the smoothness of the large tooth. He and Sam exchanged glances. A real bear's tooth.

Another call from Mrs. Lankford sent them scurrying to the meeting house. The meeting was much shorter than usual. The Reverend Checkley felt it was best for them to get on their way.

On the way home, Rob could tell his mother was concerned about what would happen to the people of the village with no doctor there to care for them. Rob didn't even want to think about it. Silently he prayed for his friend Neponset.

CHAPTER EIGHT

The City Prays

Even though North Church was only a short way from the Foy home, Josiah insisted they all ride in the carriage each Sunday morning. Rob knew that appearances were important to Josiah.

The church bells were chiming when the family climbed aboard that Sunday morning in June. Thomas and Rob sat side by side opposite Josiah and Mother. Rachel sat on her mother's lap. Rob thought his mother looked especially lovely in her new satin frock. Being summer, there was no need of a heavy cloak to cover its beauty.

As they rode along, Thomas slipped his hand between them and gave Rob a smart pinch on the leg. Rob jumped with a start and jammed his elbow into Thomas's side.

Reeling dramatically, Thomas grabbed at his side. "Ow! Now what did you do that for?" he demanded.

"Boys!" Josiah said firmly.

"He pinched me," Rob said in an attempt to defend himself.

"I didn't," Thomas retorted.

"Scoot apart," Mother suggested. "Surely the two of you can manage to get along on the Sabbath."

The seating committee had long ago designated one of the prime pews to the Foy family. It was near the front and very close to the Reverend Mather's elevated pulpit. Rob was thankful that he was separated from Thomas during the service.

Following the line singing of the psalms, the Reverend Mather, dressed in his dark clerical robes and curled powdered wig, climbed the steps up to the pulpit. Before beginning his message, he spoke of the smallpox problem.

"Governor Shute has declared a citywide day of fasting and prayer on Friday next, June 27th," he said. "I trust each of you will refrain from work that day in order to spend the time in an even more fruitful manner—in prayers before God."

The governor? Rob thought about that for a moment. If the governor called for a day of prayer and fasting, the situation must be very serious. He hoped Josiah would close the counting house for that day.

"If a member of your family," the pastor continued, "contracts this dreaded disease, please present a bill to the deacon that next Sunday. State the name of the person on the bill. These will be gathered each Sunday, and I and the deacons will pray for those who are ill and make visits as we can."

Rob wasn't sure how many times the reverend turned the large hourglass that rested on the pulpit desk, but he knew it was too many. The church grew warmer as the noonday sun crept high into the sky, and the preaching seemed endless. He was extremely relieved when the last prayer was said and Josiah opened the door to their pew box and allowed them to file out.

At their Sunday meal, Mother and Josiah discussed the upcoming day of prayer. "Will you close the counting house?" Mother asked.

"I cannot," he said simply.

Josiah had completed cutting the roast and had placed ample slices on each plate and passed them about. Rob was starved, and Freegrace cooked the best roast in all of Boston.

"But you must," Mother said gently. "It will be of utmost importance that we petition the Lord for mercy and safety for all of us."

"If this turns into an epidemic, Mary, the harbor may close. There's already talk of it. I must hurry."

"Sam Lankford says it's already an epidemic," Rob put in, "but the magistrates are keeping things quiet."

"What does Sam Lankford know?" Thomas said. "He's a South Ender."

"He happens to be at the *News Letter* every day," Rob shot back. "He knows most all the news of the city. And besides, what does it matter where a person lives?"

Thomas started to answer but Mother hushed them both. To Josiah, she said, "I know the business is important, Josiah. The money can buy many nice things. But what good is any of it if we're no longer alive to use it? Prayer for God's safekeeping would seem more important than business matters."

Josiah gave a little sigh. "Very well, my dear. Perhaps we can close the doors at lunchtime. Will that suit you?"

"Don't do it to suit me, Josiah Foy. You must be earnestly seeking God's face."

Rob marveled at his gentle mother. Her ways with Josiah were admirable. In spite of everything, he knew that Josiah cared about her very much and wanted to please her. That fact gave Rob a warm feeling inside.

Each day at the counting house, Rob did his morning chores, then reported to Mr. Vetch, who set him at the task of recording and copying. The counting room was hot, and the high stool exceedingly uncomfortable. Sharp pains shot though his back and up into his neck. Noah and Marcus, too, were set at the tasks of record keeping, but they worked in the large counting room with other clerks. Every worker took on extra work. No one was exempt.

Rob continued to run errands in the afternoons, and it was of these few moments of freedom that he dreamed all day. Whenever he could, he took his route past Dr. Boylston's apothecary shop. It only took a moment to run in and say hello.

When Rob stopped by the Thursday before the fast day, Dr. Boylston said, "Robert, I have something to show you. Can you spare the time to look?"

Of course he had the time—anything for Dr. Boylston. In his hand, the doctor held a letter from the Reverend Mather. "The reverend has heard from none of the other doctors in Boston," he confided to Rob, "and in this letter, he encourages me to use my own judgment about the inoculations. He feels it could save many lives."

"And what is your judgment, sir?"

"You know that my Dorothy has left the city with the girls."

Rob nodded. Sam had told him that the doctor's wife and daughters had left just a few days before.

"But," the doctor went on, "Tommy is still here with me." He tapped the folded letter against his palm. "The Reverend Mather's encouragement was just what I needed. Tonight I plan to inoculate Tommy and my slave, Jack, as well. And Jack's son, too, if he agrees." Dr. Boylston's son, Tommy, was only six.

"That's splendid news, sir," Rob said. "When the people see what a success it is, everyone will want to be inoculated."

"I hope so, Robert. I hope so. I ask that you keep mum about it and ask that you pray for me during your fast time tomorrow."

"Yes, sir. I will, sir."

"You're a fine friend to me, Robert."

Rob left the shop buoyed up with joy. Now perhaps Josiah would agree to have Rachel inoculated. And Rob now knew beyond a doubt that he also wanted to be inoculated.

How the city learned so quickly of those first inoculations was a mystery to Rob, but by Friday morning it was being spoken of on every street corner. On the very day when the town was to be in an attitude of prayer, Rob heard voices full of fear and anger instead.

"While all of us are striving to stop the plague," an older clerk at the counting house was saying, "this infernal doctor is spreading the stuff. It's insane."

Rob, finished with his morning chores, had just come out of the anteroom. He heard the other clerks loudly agreeing with this comment. The voices sounded almost panicky. Were they right? Would inoculations spread the smallpox? But Dr. Boylston seemed so sure. And what was anyone else doing to stop the plague?

True to his word, Josiah sent everyone home at noon. He then invited Rob to ride home in the carriage. Rob much preferred walking, but he politely accepted.

As they jostled along, Rob dared to bring up the subject of Dr. Boylston. Of course, Josiah had already heard the gossip.

"He didn't begin the operations with strangers," Rob pointed out. "He began with his very own son and his faithful slave, Jack. That shows his confidence in the operation."

"It shows only one thing to me," Josiah said as he gazed out the side window. "That he's a raving lunatic. He's gone completely mad. And because of his demented thinking, he's putting the entire community in danger."

"But, sir, what if he's right?"

"A more thought-provoking question is, what if he's wrong? Which I'm sure he is. If he were right, all the physicians would be siding with him. None has done so."

"Sir, I believe Rachel should be inoculated."

"You've asked that before, and I emphatically say no. Never would I risk her life in such a crude manner."

"Then what about me?"

"What about you?"

"Let me be inoculated."

Josiah turned to Rob with a stunned look of disbelief. "You're talking about suicide, Robert. Put it out of your mind this instant. We'll not talk of it further."

Since Latin School was recessed for the summer, Thomas was already there when they arrived at the house. Rachel sat at the table eating a bowl of hasty pudding. She was too small to join in the fasting. Freegrace prepared mugs of cider for the rest of the family, after which Josiah gathered them all in his study.

"We will go to our separate bedchambers for prayer and Scripture study this afternoon," he instructed. "This evening, after the chores are completed, we will gather back here in my study for prayers."

Rob's stomach was already rumbling and he wondered how he would make it through the afternoon with no food, but he made a diligent effort to study in his psalter. Later, he sat by his window, praying about the inoculations and particularly asking the Lord to protect Dr. Boylston.

As he prayed, he saw something moving about near the kitchen garden. It couldn't be Freegrace, for she was in her room praying just as the family members were. Looking again, Rob recognized Thomas! The younger boy skulked along the brambles where the berry bushes grew, glanced about him, and then made his way into the garden. Although Rob couldn't be sure, it looked as though Thomas was enjoying a little feast of early summer vegetables. Perhaps a few tender sweet carrots.

Rob jumped up from the window seat, ready to run downstairs and tell Josiah. Finally he had his chance to get even with Thomas for the mean things he'd been doing lately.

At the door, he paused, remembering the Scripture Dr. Boylston quoted about overcoming evil with good. Slowly he walked back across the room and sat down in the window seat. Rob rubbed at his own empty stomach. If he'd thought of the garden first, he might have been sneaking down there himself!

With his mind more at peace, Rob thought to pray about his situation at the counting house. "If you please, Lord," he prayed, "I'm trying to be the best ship merchant I know how to be, but I'm certain I'd be a much better doctor. It seems a little selfish to be praying for me when there's so much sadness in the city. But Mr. Vetch suggested I pray about the situation, so I am. And Lord," he added, "I think maybe Dr. Boylston's praying for me as well, and I know You hear and answer his prayers!"

CHAPTER NINE

Attack on Dr. Boylston

July arrived and with it the heat of summer. Nearly six weeks had passed since the Reverend Cotton Mather had written to the physicians. At last they held a meeting, but it resulted in their condemning the smallpox inoculations. The physicians' joint conclusion was that "inoculation in Boston is likely to prove of dangerous consequence." The statement was published in the *Boston News Letter*.

Rob first saw the physicians' statement at the print shop before the paper was ever distributed. He could hardly believe this new development. Among the most vocal of the doctors was William Douglass, a close friend of Josiah Foy's.

"This is terrible," he told Sam. "This could set Josiah's mind more firmly than ever against Dr. Boylston."

"And if this can sway someone like your stepfather," Sam said, "think of the effect it will have on others in the city. I wouldn't want to be in Dr. Boylston's shoes right now."

Even Mr. Campbell seemed concerned about the doctors' statement.

"I'm going to go tell Dr. Boylston," Rob said.

"Here," Mr. Campbell thrust the sheet of paper into his hands. "Take this copy so he can see for himself. And tell him. . ." He paused a moment, running his hand over his wispy gray hair. "Tell him we're praying for him."

"Yes, sir, I certainly will."

Rob ran from the print shop to the apothecary shop in Dock Square with the folded paper rustling inside his shirt. But when Rob showed the article to his friend, Dr. Boylston seemed not at all concerned.

"Each man is entitled to his own opinion, Robert," he said, "even when his opinion is wrong."

"But sir, aren't you bothered about this condemnation?"

The doctor smiled. "Come here, Robert."

Robert followed him into the back room of the shop where six-year-old Tommy was playing on the floor with a set of toy soldiers. Tommy looked up and waved. "Hello, Rob," he said. "Can you come play with me?"

Rob hadn't seen Tommy since before the inoculation, but it

was obvious that the boy was as fit as a fiddle. "Is he all right?" Rob asked.

"He's fine," Dr. Boylston answered. "And so is Jack and his son, Jackie. They were sick for a few days, but it was mild. Now they're well. I'm keeping Tommy here by himself for a few days, just in case."

"It's like a miracle," Rob said.

"Definitely a miracle," Dr. Boylston agreed.

"Robert, will you play?" Tommy asked again.

"Not now, Tommy. I must get back to the counting house."

Doctor Boylston closed the door and turned to Rob. He rattled the paper in his hand. "Now do you see why this doesn't disturb me? It doesn't matter to me what they say."

"If only Josiah could see Tommy, then perhaps he'd agree to allow us to be inoculated."

"Don't be too sure, Robert. People are funny. Sometimes when a person's mind is made up, even what they see with their own eyes is not proof enough to change their minds."

After leaving the shop, Rob began to think of ways to convince Josiah to allow the inoculations. If Dr. Boylston was right, then it was going to take some doing. First, the timing would have to be right. But as the days passed, the perfect opportunity never presented itself.

Within a week came a fiery article in the *News Letter* personally attacking Dr. Boylston. The article called Dr. Boylston ignorant, illiterate, and incapable of understanding the inoculation. It went on to accuse the doctor not only of negligence, but also of spreading the infection.

The name beneath the article was "William Philantropos," but everyone knew it had been written by Dr. Douglass. The evening it appeared, Josiah pointed out the article to Rob, saying, "See here, young Robert? This is what educated men say about your Dr. Boylston."

The family was gathered in Josiah's study for evening prayers before retiring to bed. Rachel was curled contentedly on Mother's lap, and Thomas and Robert were seated on the rug. Kitty purred loudly as she slept near Mother's feet. Freegrace sat a ways apart from the family, her busy fingers darning one of the boys' stockings.

Rob, of course, had learned of the article the day before, and it had infuriated him. There was no basis for the slander, since Dr. Boylston had performed many successful surgeries both in Boston and in outlying towns. But before he could speak in Dr. Boylston's defense, Josiah continued.

"In case you were not aware, Dr. Douglass received his education from three different universities in England and Europe. Dr. Boylston knows only what he learned from his backwoods father." He jabbed a finger at the paper. "See that word 'negligence'? Do you realize the danger that negligence can cause? No one in Boston will be safe if he continues."

"How can anyone know if he's being negligent?" Rob asked, fighting to keep the anger from his voice. "He invited all the doctors to come and view his patients, but all refuse."

Josiah smacked the folded paper smartly across his knee, making a pop. "And who are you to question the learned men of this profession?" he demanded. "I'm sure they have perfectly good reasons for their actions. I certainly wouldn't want any of them telling me how to run my shipping concern."

Mother leaned over to Josiah's chair, handing him the Bible. "Isn't it time for Scripture reading?" she asked gently, which politely closed the conversation.

After prayers, the children were dismissed to leave the room and go upstairs. Rachel scooped Kitty up in her arms and kissed her mother goodnight. Since it was summer and still light, there was no need for carrying lamps with them. As Freegrace went to put her darning away, she said to Rachel, "You go on upstairs with the boys. I'll be along shortly."

Although it wasn't fully dark, there were shadows in the back stairs that went up from the kitchen, making it scary for Rachel. "Hold my hand, please, Robert," she said reaching out.

As Thomas bounded up the stairs ahead of them, Robert slowed down to assist Rachel. Since Kitty was weighing her down, she couldn't maneuver the narrow stairs easily.

They paused at the landing as she shifted Kitty's weight and managed a better hold. At the top of the stairs, Thomas suddenly leaped out from the shadows making a grotesque face.

"Aha!" he shouted. "I am Dr. Dunderhead Boylston. I'm going to cut the cat and inoculate her!" With that, he grabbed Kitty and lifted her above his head. The cat yowled, and Rachel screamed.

"Give Kitty back to me," she cried.

"Yes, yes," Thomas crooned, still making a wicked face. "A willing victim for my experiment." In his free hand he waved a large darning needle as though he were going to jab it into the kitten.

By now Rachel was frantic. She was pulling at Thomas, begging him not to hurt Kitty.

"But I'm going to save her life. Ha ha. Just like the ignorant, illiterate Dr. Boylston."

"Give her the cat," Rob insisted.

"Just look who's giving orders," Thomas said, still holding the

84

crying cat aloft. "It's the ragamuffin South Ender. If it weren't for my father, you'd be living down there among all the rest of the—"

At that moment, Kitty was able to flip around and dig her sharp claws into Thomas's hand. He recoiled, flinging the cat down. Fur puffed out, the frightened cat tore wildly down the darkened hall with Rachel hard on its heels.

Rob took a step toward Thomas. "Only cowards pick on little girls," he said.

"But you're the one who cheats at horse racing," Thomas countered. He held up the large darning needle. "You take another step toward me, and I'll use this on you instead of on that silly old cat."

"You do and you'll rue the day." Rob faked a jump forward, which caused Thomas to lunge. As he did, Rob easily and quickly side stepped. Spinning around, he forcefully grabbed the hand holding the needle and began to twist. The pain set Thomas to squalling.

"Drop it," Rob ordered.

"Let me go," Thomas yelled.

"What's all this caterwauling up here?" said a voice from down the hall. It was Josiah. The carpet had muffled his steps up the front stairs.

Rob felt Thomas's hand go limp and saw the silvery needle fall to the floor. He moved to put his foot over it. "We were just playing," Rob answered. "Just playing."

Josiah was carrying the small whale oil lamp from his study desk. "That's the noisiest playing I've ever heard. It sounds more like Indians painted up for an attack." He lifted the lamp higher as he approached and studied their faces.

"We were just playing," Thomas echoed weakly.

"Mm hm. I see."

Just then, Rachel emerged from a guest bedroom down the hall. "I found Kitty," she called out. She stopped short when she saw Josiah hovering over the boys.

As Josiah turned around to look at her, Rob put his finger to his mouth, motioning her to keep quiet.

"Rachel," said Josiah, "what was all the noise up here?"

Shadows from the lamp played on Rachel's dark curls as she gave Rob a long, intense look. Slowly, Rob shook his head. "Kitty got away," she said in a soft whisper.

As Josiah turned back around to the boys, Rob quickly dropped his hand. "All right, all right," Josiah said. "So you two were playing, and she was chasing her cat."

The three children nodded vigorously.

"What's the trouble, sir?" Freegrace asked as she came up the back stairs and surveyed the scene.

"The trouble is, we can't seem to turn our backs on these children. Everyone go to bed now!" he ordered.

As Josiah turned to go, Freegrace swished by in her long skirts to take Rachel to bed. Robert seized the moment to reach down undetected and grab the darning needle, then scurried to his room. In the morning, he'd slip the needle back into Freegrace's mending basket without being noticed.

After removing his outer garments and pulling on his nightshirt, Rob sat for a long time at his open window, thinking. He kept wondering what he would have done to Thomas had Josiah not come up the stairs. His anger was still set on a very short fuse.

Long after Rob had crawled into bed and had fallen asleep, he was awakened by the tolling of the bells at North Church. He knew by the sound that they were not alarm bells, but funeral bells. Someone with smallpox must have died. In spite of the warmth of the summer night, he shivered beneath his coverlet.

The funeral bells pealed more often as the month of July progressed. Sometimes in the night Rob could hear the "dead cart," as it rumbled through the streets. The selectmen traveled from house to house to take a toll of how many cases had been reported. By the end of July there were nearly two hundred cases of smallpox in Boston. No one knew who would be next to get sick.

One morning as Rob was finishing his breakfast, Mother came to tell him she and Mrs. Lankford would be taking supplies to Punkapaog the next Saturday. Rob brightened at the prospect until he was told he must stay home.

"Is Sam going?" he asked.

His mother shook her head.

"But why? Why should you and Mrs. Lankford go without us?"

"It's too dangerous now, Robert. There's no reason for us to take the chance. We may not be able to go again, but we're going to take blankets and supplies. We'll only stay long enough to unload the supplies."

"But it's not right that you go alone. I want to be with you."

"Moseley will be with us."

Rob wanted to protest, to make her take him, but it was useless to argue when her mind was made up.

"Your Aunt Beth has been helping us collect a few items. You're to stop by there and fetch them before coming home this evening."

"Yes, ma'am." He couldn't look at her.

Mother crossed over to him and put her arms about his shoulders. "Trust God, Robert. Everything will be all right."

Although he was much too old to be fussed over like a baby, it felt wonderful to be held even for a moment. "Yes, ma'am. I'll try."

That day, two of the tall desks in the counting room remained unoccupied. Both young men had come down with smallpox.

CHAPTER TEN

Uncle Nathan Takes a Risk

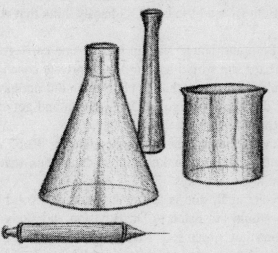

When Robert arrived at the toy shop the next afternoon, he found Aunt Beth and Uncle Nathan in the back room. They were seated at the table, reading a letter from Uncle William. Rob's Uncle William lived in Cambridge with his wife and two young daughters.

After Rob was welcomed and made comfortable with a cup of tea, his aunt shared the letter. Mostly it was news of Uncle William's family and his good job as an accountant for a law firm there. But the purpose of the letter was to invite Beth to come and stay until the smallpox scare was over.

When she folded the letter, they sat quietly for a moment. "Are you going, Aunt Beth?" Rob managed to say. He couldn't imagine the toy shop without her.

Before she could answer, Uncle Nathan spoke up. "Of course she's going. If I have to carry her there on my back." He reached across the table to take his wife's hand.

Aunt Beth gave a little laugh. "I hardly think that will be necessary."

Aunt Beth and Uncle Nathan had no fine carriage as Josiah had. Perhaps she would have to take a private coach. But even that would cost money that Uncle Nathan did not have.

"Why don't you just go to Dr. Boylston and get an inoculation?" Rob asked.

His aunt and uncle glanced at one another. "Rob," Aunt Beth said gently, "don't you know how dangerous that is? Why everyone in Boston says—"

"Everyone in Boston is just plain ignorant," Rob blurted out. "If they would but listen to Dr. Boylston and study what he's doing, then they would see." Realizing his voice was rising in the quiet little shop, he stopped. "I'm sorry," he said. "I didn't mean to lash out at the two of you."

"Mercy me," said Aunt Beth, "I had no idea your feelings were so strong in the matter."

"I'm here to pick up the supplies for Mother. I'd best get them and be on my way."

When Aunt Beth stood up to fetch the bag, Rob realized she looked different. He'd not seen her for several weeks, and his mother had not told him—but now he realized Aunt Beth was going to have a baby. No wonder Uncle Nathan wanted to get her away from the city. Certainly she shouldn't risk an inoculation.

Aunt Beth was shaking her head as she brought the large bag to him. "I cannot understand why Mary insists on going back to the village at this time."

Rob certainly agreed with her. "She and Mrs. Lankford have refused to allow Sam or me to go along."

"And you're worried about her, am I right?" asked Uncle Nathan.

Robert could only nod.

"Well buck up there, young chap. How about if I go along with them? I can lend a hand and make sure the ladies stay out of harm's way."

"Oh would you, Uncle Nathan? I'd be ever so grateful. Did you know," he confided to them, "that Mother has received an invitation to stay for a time with Aunt Esther in Roxbury, but she won't go?"

"Mary's so strong-willed," said Aunt Beth.

"Stubborn is more like it," agreed Uncle Nathan. "If the opportunity presents itself, perhaps I can talk to her about the subject as we travel."

"I doubt that," Rob said, "since Mrs. Lankford will be along. Mother would never dream of leaving Boston if Mrs. Lankford couldn't go."

"He's right," Aunt Beth said. "Mother and Phoebe are very close friends."

Nathan, always the optimist, said, "Still and yet, I shall do what I can."

As Rob left the shop, he realized he still had time to run over to the *News Letter* before going home for supper. Even though the bag was heavy and the stop would be out of his way, he needed to talk to Sam. Perhaps Sam could talk their mothers out of going to Punkapaog. The subject, however, was quickly forgotten when he stepped inside the shop.

"Robert," Sam called out, "come take a look at this. You can scarce believe your eyes."

"What is it?" Rob dropped the bag by the door and rushed to where Sam and Mr. Campbell were working by the large press.

From a nearby table Sam picked up a broadside that was similar in form to the *News Letter*, but it wasn't a paper Rob recognized.

Aloud Rob read the name at the top. "The *Boston Courant*? A new paper in town?"

"New and vicious," put in Mr. Campbell.

"Look at the editor's name," Sam told him.

"James Franklin?" He looked at Sam. "Ben's brother?"

Sam nodded. "And can you believe, Benjamin is an apprentice now for his brother."

"He attended your school, didn't he?"

"Ben was in the upper grades when I started, but I recall him as being a kindhearted soul, gentle to all of us smaller boys." Sam shook his head in disbelief. "Now this."

Rob scanned the page and quickly saw that nearly every column was an attack against inoculation and specifically against Dr. Boylston. "How can this be? Why would the Franklins do this?"

"Perhaps controversy sells more subscriptions than news," suggested Mr. Campbell with a sigh. He leaned heavily against the printing press and suddenly appeared to be very weary.

"Can we put a stop to it?" Rob asked. Somehow he wanted to help Mr. Campbell and Dr. Boylston. "Is no one defending the inoculations?"

"We do have a bit of encouragement in that area," Sam said. "The Reverend Mather and several other of the clergy have written an article in support." He ran his fingers through his mop of red hair. "As much good as it will do after all this."

"I wonder why Dr. Boylston doesn't speak out in defense of himself?" Rob said.

"Perhaps," Mr. Campbell said as he motioned to Sam to re-ink the type, "it's because he's too busy doing what he knows to be right."

The clatter of the press as the two went back to work gave Rob his leave. Rob had much to think about as he walked homeward carrying the heavy bag in the August heat.

Uncle Nathan was as good as his word. Not only did he travel to the praying town with Mother and Mrs. Lankford, but he also saw to it that they stayed far from any of the Indians who were infected with smallpox. When he later reported this news to Rob, Rob thanked him profusely. Uncle Nathan's generosity gave Rob an idea.

Before starting his work at the counting house one morning, Rob asked Josiah if he could speak to him.

"I'm extremely busy," Josiah said. And it was true. Rob had never seen such a flurry of activity as there had been at the Foy Shipping Lines that summer. "Is it important?" his stepfather wanted to know.

"It is very important," Rob replied.

"Speak quickly then." He laid down his quill and looked up to where Rob stood before his desk.

"You're aware, sir, that my Uncle Nathan accompanied mother to the praying town on Saturday past."

"I am aware. It was good of him to do so."

"Yes, sir. He took good care of her."

"Yes. So?"

"There is a way you could show your appreciation to Uncle Nathan."

"I'm to show my appreciation? What is it you're asking, Robert?"

Rob cleared his throat. This wasn't as easy as he'd thought. "Aunt Beth is. . .I mean she needs to go away. Uncle William has invited her to Cambridge, and Uncle Nathan wants her to go, but they. . .Well, sir, they have no money."

"And you want me to pay her coach fare?"

"Oh no, sir. I just thought Moseley could take her to Cambridge in the carriage. In your carriage, I mean."

Josiah was quiet, and Rob could see he was considering the idea.

"She's going to have a baby, and it's urgent that she go."

"Very well, Robert. We shall do this for your Aunt Beth." He paused a moment. "I'm certain it would make your mother very pleased."

"Oh yes, sir. I'm sure of that."

"I shall excuse you to run and tell her to prepare to leave tomorrow morning at dawn. Then go tell Moseley the plan. It's good of you," he added, "to be concerned for others."

Rob's heart was soaring. At least Aunt Beth now would be safe.

"Step quickly, Robert. I expect you back here to put in as many hours as you can before quitting time."

"Yes, sir!" he called back as he sped out the door.

As happy as Rob was about his plan, he failed to realize what a tearful parting it would cause. Mother, Rob, and Rachel rode the carriage to Uncle Nathan and Aunt Beth's house very early the next morning. They wanted to help with the loading as well as tell Aunt Beth goodbye.

Rob had expected his mother to be in tears, but seeing Uncle Nathan cry made tears well up in Rob's eyes as well. He tried to blink them back, but they just kept running down his cheeks as if they had a mind of their own. He kept wiping them away with the sleeve of his silk waistcoat, but more came in their place.

After the carriage had clattered off with Beth still waving out the window, Nathan turned to Mother. "Now we need to get you off to Roxbury as soon as Moseley returns," he said. Uncle Nathan hadn't bothered to wipe his tears away, and his eyes were red and puffy.

Rob's mother shook her head. "I'm where I'm supposed to be for the time being," she told him.

Uncle Nathan looked at Rob and gave a shrug.

"Rachel and I will be getting on home," Mother continued. "If we leave now, we should be there before the sun becomes too warm." She straightened her new bonnet and fluffed out her long skirts. She tucked her tear-dampened kerchief into her glove. "Come, Rachel." She held out her hand and Rachel grabbed it.

Turning back to Uncle Nathan, Mother added, "We'd be pleased to have you come to supper one day soon."

"I accept your kind invitation, Mary."

She took a few more steps, and then added, "If I can be of help in the shop, please let me know."

"Yes, I will. Thank you."

To Rob she said, "Get yourself on down to the counting house now, and don't dally along the way."

"I'm going." But the sad feeling inside of Rob made his feet want to drag rather than hurry.

When Mother and Rachel were well down the street, Uncle Nathan said, "May I cut you a slice of brown bread to eat on your way to Long Wharf?"

"Thank you, but I've had my breakfast."

"But a boy is always hungry, am I right?"

Rob didn't feel much like eating, but he wanted to be polite. So he nodded and followed Uncle Nathan into their neat little cottage. The place seemed hollow and empty without Aunt Beth's happy voice.

Uncle Nathan took down the loaf of bread from the shelf, along with the knife. "Something tells me you were behind this loan of the fine carriage, Robert Junior." Uncle Nathan stopped slicing and gave Rob a warm smile. "I'll forever be grateful to you."

Rob felt tongue-tied. "It was nothing really." He wondered how Uncle Nathan found out.

"You're a compassionate young man," Uncle Nathan went on, embarrassing Rob even more. "But I have something else to tell you." He placed the thick slice of bread in Rob's outstretched palm. "I listened to your strong remarks when you were here the other day."

"My strong remarks?"

"About Dr. Boylston's inoculation operation. My curiosity was keenly aroused, so I went to his shop to talk to him."

"You did?" Rob was surprised. He never thought he could persuade anyone about anything.

"The doctor is coming here this evening to perform the operation."

Rob nearly dropped his bread. Part of him was a little frightened. The other part of him was terribly excited.

"Beth's leaving made the timing perfect. I'm going to lock up the shop for several days, and I don't want you coming around until I'm all better. Tell your mother I cannot accept the supper invitation, much as I would like to. I didn't feel she was quite ready to hear this news."

"Oh no, sir, she's not ready. Josiah has talked against it from the very beginning. In this matter, Mother seems unwilling to disagree with him."

"Very well then, be off with you. And remember to say a prayer for me."

"Oh yes, I will. Thank you for telling me, Uncle Nathan. You can trust Dr. Boylston."

"I plan to do just that, Robert Junior!"

CHAPTER ELEVEN

A Fight with Ben Franklin

The funeral bells pealed almost constantly, and the death wagons went to and fro with greater frequency. Here and there throughout the city, businesses stood empty either because of families leaving or because entire families were too ill to work. At church on Sundays the number of bills handed in to the deacons increased in frightening numbers. By the first week in October, the *News Letter* reported over two thousand total cases of smallpox.

A sharp nip of fall filled the air as Rob carried water to the livestock. The cows had dried up, so Freegrace did no more milking. The first frost had sent Mother and Freegrace scurrying to harvest what they could of what remained in the kitchen garden. Squash, pumpkins, and turnips were stored in the root cellar. Apples were cut in sections and hung up to dry. Bouquets of herbs were dried, tied in bunches, and strung up in the kitchen, giving the place an aroma of tangy spices.

Sometimes when Rob was home and events seemed so normal, he tried to forget that the epidemic raged all about him. He rarely saw Dr. Boylston these days. Every doctor in Boston was working day and night in a frustrated effort to help the sick and dying. Thankfully, Uncle Nathan's inoculation was a success. He and Rob rejoiced together. But in spite of Dr. Boylston's successes, the fear and distrust of the inoculations continued to grow. The "pamphlet war" raged right alongside the terrible epidemic.

The two young clerks from the shipping line both died of smallpox. Their tall stools stood vacant. There was no reason for Josiah to hire new workers since Boston Harbor was quarantined. The panicky rush that existed at Foy Shipping Lines throughout the summer dwindled and then disappeared. A spirit of quiet gloom hovered over the counting house, as indeed it hung over all of Boston.

When Rob walked into the counting room that morning, he tried not to look at those empty places. Mr. Goddard had come down with the pox as well, and Mr. Vetch was doing his work.

"How is Mr. Goddard faring?" Rob asked Mr. Vetch when the older man arrived.

Mr. Vetch adjusted his gold spectacles and peered over them at Rob. "Not well, Master Robert. Not well. I've seen the smallpox come to Boston in my days, but nothing of the likes of this."

Rob was never so grateful to be sent on errands, even though the streets were almost empty of traffic. The wharves were ghostly quiet. But it was still good to get out. Mr. Vetch seemed to understand. There were some afternoons when he sent Rob out for things of very little importance. Or if there were two deliveries, he'd allow Rob to make them in two trips. Neither of them ever discussed the matter, but both knew the secret.

That afternoon, gray clouds had gathered in the harbor and the wind off the water was sharply colder. When he stepped outside on his way to the *News Letter* office, Rob wondered if the first snow of the season would fall before dusk. He pulled his hat down against the wind and snugged up the collar of his greatcoat.

Mr. Campbell had more issues of the *Courant* ready to show Rob when he arrived. The Franklins seemed to be making a great deal of money off the controversy over the inoculations.

"Some of this fury might have quieted down had the Franklins let it rest," Mr. Campbell said as Rob scanned the newest broadside. "A fire with no fuel will soon die out."

"One would think the citizens of Boston would be too busy or too ill to bother with such things." Rob laid the page back on Mr. Campbell's desk.

"I agree, and yet the anger is raging as never before." Mr. Campbell leaned back in his chair. "Dr. Boylston was called before the magistrates yesterday."

"Again?"

"Again. I believe this makes the third time they've ordered him to stop the inoculations."

Rob shook his head in wonder. "Don't they know they can never stop him? He's the most determined man I've ever met."

"And yet free of malice," Mr. Campbell added.

"Yes, free of malice," Rob echoed. That was the part Rob couldn't understand. With all those adversaries fighting him, Dr. Boylston showed no hint of wanting revenge against anyone. Rob continued to be amazed. The doctor even refused to write a report and publish it.

"The time is not yet," he told Rob one day. "The reports will be written, but not until all this is over and men's tempers have cooled."

"And where is Sam today?" Rob asked, realizing his friend hadn't come bounding into the midst of their conversation.

Mr. Campbell nodded toward the back. "Stirring up a batch of ink. Our supply of flaxseed oil is low. If everything continues as it is in the city, we may be hard pressed to find new supplies."

Rob had already heard of items being in short supply. Farmers from outlying districts were no longer bringing their products into the city to sell. And, of course, the slowdown of the shipping also caused shortages.

"May I visit with Sam?" Rob asked, wanting to get away from all the depressing news.

Mr. Campbell waved his arm. "Be off. He's just started, so he'll be there a while."

Rob hurried out to where Sam was stirring the ink. "You're thankful for the fire today, I'll wager," he said.

Sam looked up from his work and gave Rob a friendly wave and a smile. "That I am." Sam had shed his coat, but he had a woolen muffler tied over his ears and his hat on over the muffler. "At least one side of me is keeping warm. I've not figured out a method where I can turn around backward and still stir."

Rob laughed out loud. It felt so good to laugh in the midst of all the sorrow. "That would be a jolly good trick. If you perfect it, I want to be the first to watch."

Just then Sam's expression changed as he saw something over Rob's shoulder. "Look there," Sam said almost in a whisper. Rob turned to see an older boy walking between the shops on Spring Lane. "That's Ben Franklin."

"Are you sure?" Rob asked.

"That's him."

Rob grabbed the pole from Sam's hands and threw it to the ground. "Sam, run out there and fake him out. I'll go the other way. Make sure he follows you down Water Street, then duck behind Anchor Tavern. That's where I'll be waiting. Let's give him what for!"

Sam's blue eyes lit up. "Let's get him!"

Rob never saw how Sam got Ben to chase him down Water Street, but he probably smacked him a good one from behind and then ran. Rob crouched down behind the tavern, which was quiet at this hour. Within moments Sam sped by. As he did, Rob sprang from his hiding place, tripping Ben and sending him face first onto the cold ground.

When Sam heard the commotion behind him, he spun about and was beside Rob in a wink. Together they piled on top of Ben, pinning him to the ground.

"What is this? Two against one is hardly a fair fight," Ben said as he struggled against their strong grip. Although Ben was sixteen, his slight build made holding him quite easy.

"Who are you to talk about a fair fight, you holder of the poison pen?" Sam said.

"What are you talking about? Say, aren't you Samuel Lankford?" Ben pulled and struggled again but saw it was useless and lay still. "Little redhaired Samuel. So what brings you to jumping people in the alleyways? Is this how far you've advanced since your days at writing school? And who's your accomplice?"

The older boy's nonchalant attitude made Rob fume. "Your rotten newspaper and your underhanded way of inciting mistrust and fear has caused nothing but grief in this city." Rob wanted to punch his nose, but it seemed pretty cowardly since Ben was just lying there talking.

"I regret to inform you vigilantes, but the *Courant* is not my newspaper. Nor would I want it to be. It belongs to my older brother, James."

"But you work for him," Rob said. "You're part of the grand assault."

"No need for you boys to get in a huff at me. Granted, I spend long hours at the compositing bench, and I'm pretty fast, if I do say so myself. But the type I set is none of my own words. Ah, that they were. I'd love to write."

His calm response was taking the fire out of both Rob and Sam. They looked at one another, and Sam nodded. "Let's let him up."

Sam reached out to help Ben to his feet and then dusted off the back of Ben's coat, which was as plain as Rob's was fancy. "Sorry," Sam said meekly. "No hard feelings?" He picked up Ben's hat from the ground.

"Hard feelings seem to abound these days." Ben grabbed his hat and replaced it on his head. "I guess I have none, but you both seem to have a few."

"Dr. Zabdiel Boylston is my close friend," Rob spoke up.

"I see," Ben said thoughtfully. "And who might you be?"

"Robert Allerton, Junior."

"You're the doctor's apprentice, I assume?"

Rob shook his head. "I'm apprenticed to my stepfather, Josiah Foy."

"Of course. The Foy Shipping Lines. That explains the dandy silk and ruffles." He reached out and fluffed the ruffles hanging from Rob's neckband.

Rob was suddenly ashamed of his fine clothes. But he couldn't

forget why they'd cornered Ben in the first place. "Is there nothing you can do to stop these ruthless attacks against Dr. Boylston?
He's been called before the magistrates three times now. The pub-
lic rage against him is fueled by your brother's cruel paper."

"Answer me a question, young Robert Allerton, Junior. Do
you tell your stepfather how to run his merchant business?"

"No, of course not."

"You see? Likewise, I have no power over James. But tell me,
I've been quite curious about the inoculation. Can you explain
it to me?"

Briefly Rob told him how the operation was performed and
gave a few details of the successful cases—especially his own
Uncle Nathan.

"Amazing," Ben said. "What a fascinating concept. I should
like to meet your Dr. Boylston some day. Now, if you please, I
must be on my way." He tipped his tricorn hat and smiled. "It
was a delight, uh, running into you today." With that, he gave a
little chuckle.

"Well, Robert," Sam said after Ben was gone, "you did it
again. Acting before you think."

Rob gave a shrug. "Perhaps we could have handled it differently, but it was still important that we talk to him."

"Good gracious!" Sam yelped. "My ink!"

Rob could hardly keep up with his friend as Sam sprinted back
to the dooryard of the *News Letter*. There was Mr. Campbell stirring the ink. "Welcome home, Sam. The next time, would you
please ask permission before leaving the fire and the ink unat-
tended?"

Even though Mr. Campbell seldom grew angry, Rob knew
Sam felt badly about running off. It was similar to how Rob felt

when he disappointed his mother.

"Sorry, Mr. Campbell. We saw James Franklin's younger brother and we ran after him."

"Hm, I see." Mr. Campbell handed the stir stick to Sam. "And did you solve all the problems of Boston by attacking young Ben?"

Rob felt his face burn. "No, sir, we didn't solve anything. Ben said he has nothing to do with what his brother prints in the *Courant.*"

"I can't say I'm surprised. From what I've heard, the two brothers are leagues apart in thought and person."

"He said he'd like to meet Dr. Boylston," Sam put in.

"Now wouldn't that be an odd twist," mused Mr. Campbell as he moved to go back inside.

"What would be, sir?" Rob wanted to know.

"If Ben became interested in the inoculation operation. Or better yet, if he actually received the inoculation." With that he went in and closed the door.

Rob looked at Sam. "Now that is an interesting thought. Wonder how we could work that?"

Sam shook his head. "If you have any more harebrained notions, I'll thank you to keep them to yourself. I was addled enough to follow you a moment ago, but I hope to use better sense next time. Now help me get this kettle inside. It's the least you can do."

Rob helped Sam put a pole through the kettle handle and hoist it up and into the shop. After the fire had been put out, Rob left for Long Wharf. Tiny delicate flakes of snow were beginning to sift down all across the quiet city.

As he hurried through the cold, Rob began to regret his hasty actions with Ben. How he longed to have control over his anger. A gentle sort of chap, Ben seemed unwilling to fight back. Rob didn't dare think what he would have done if the situation had been reversed. Just before he turned onto Long Wharf, Rob saw that he'd marred his shoes and had torn a hole in his white silk knee stockings in the scuffle with Ben. If Josiah saw it, Rob would most certainly be in trouble—again.

Back at the counting house Mr. Vetch met him at the door to inform him that Mr. Goddard had died. The news gave Rob a sick feeling in his stomach. Josiah's office door was closed, and not even Mr. Vetch was allowed in.

"Your father is greatly distressed" was all Mr. Vetch would say.

Josiah Foy, the man who was always brimming with poise and confidence—Rob could not perceive him being so downcast he would close himself in his office. These were strange times.

CHAPTER TWELVE
Saying Goodbye

In a typical year, early November meant the citywide holiday of Election Day. Citizens gathered in the common for speeches, good food, and a lively array of games. However, 1721 was not a typical year. The elections were canceled. There'd been much talk on Sam's part to enter Rob and Abrecan in one of the many races, but it was not to be.

The day in November when the doors to the Foy Shipping Lines actually closed had started out as a regular workday. Late that morning, Josiah called all the employees and apprentices into the main counting room to tell them the news. Rob could hardly believe how their numbers had dwindled.

"I had hoped," Josiah said to his small group, "that we could hang on and weather this storm. I hoped I could continue to keep you in my employ. However, we are up against great odds. Not only are we in the throes of a major epidemic—and now facing winter—but now the harbor is closed."

As Rob watched, he thought he saw tears glistening in his stepfather's eyes. The decision to close must have been extremely difficult for Josiah. Rob swallowed over a lump in his own throat. His heart was saddened for those who were sick and dying and also now for those who were out of work.

Josiah spoke slowly and chose his words carefully. "Some of our ships won't be aware until they sail into port that they cannot dock. They will be adversely affected as well. This predicament is difficult for everyone."

He paced to and fro before them, tapping his pearl-handled cane lightly as he stepped. "Just as soon as this adversity has passed—and mark my word, it will pass—I shall retain all of you once again. We shall pick up where we left off, and we'll grow to be greater than ever."

Sniffling sounded from the back of the room. Rob turned to see that it was Noah. Suddenly Rob realized that Noah truly loved this place as much as Rob despised it.

Josiah closed the short meeting with a prayer for safety and God's protection for all. Then one by one they filed out until there was only Josiah, Mr. Vetch, and Rob remaining.

Mr. Vetch and Rob extinguished the fires that Rob had laid that morning. When he had arrived before dawn, Rob had no idea that Josiah was planning to close. Nothing had been said.

"That's it, sir," said Mr. Vetch. "We're ready to go."

"Thank you, Mr. Vetch." Josiah opened the front door, and the three were met with a gust of frigid air. Once they were outside, he turned to place the key into the lock and give it a turn.

As if on cue, Mr. Moseley pulled up in Josiah's carriage. Rob realized that at least Mr. Moseley had been taken into Josiah's confidence. Josiah reached out to shake Mr. Vetch's hand, they said quick goodbyes, and then Mr. Vetch hurried down Long Wharf on his way home.

"Will you ride home with me?" Josiah asked Rob.

"If you please, sir. I would like your permission to go to Dock Square—to Dr. Boylston's."

Josiah recoiled for a moment. Rob knew he was still very much against the inoculations, even though the success reports were increasing over the past weeks and months. Then Josiah's shoulders dropped and he gave a tired sigh. "Yes, very well. You may go. I suppose if you're there, you will at least be out of mischief."

Rob was sure his heart was going to explode right there.

"Shall we give you a ride?" Moseley called down from the driver's seat.

"Oh no. No thank you." Rob took off in a dead run all the way to Dock Square.

Rob wasn't surprised that Dr. Boylston was not in his shop. He was constantly out on calls. Rob hung his coat and hat on the wooden pegs in the back room. The fire in the fireplace was nearly out. From the woodshed in back, he brought in two large logs, placed them on the dying fire, and stacked kindling on and around them. Soon the cheery flames were leaping and dancing, lighting up the room and giving off warmth.

He filled the kettle with water and placed it near the fire. As soon as the doctor arrived, Rob could quickly brew tea for him. Next, he took the birch broom and swept out the entire shop and the back room. He knew he should be saddened that the counting house was closed, but his heart was singing.

Before the morning was out, Rob heard the front door open. He stepped from the back room and was surprised to see Sam standing there. "I thought I'd find you here," his friend said as he took off his hat and loosened his muffler. "I went all the way to the counting house, but I saw the door was locked."

Rob came closer to his friend. His face was different. Something was wrong. "Why were you looking for me?" Rob asked.

"To tell you. . ." Sam pressed a fist to his eye to stop the tears. "Mother's come down with the smallpox."

"No. Not Mrs. Lankford." A strange numbness coursed through Rob's body. "Sam," he whispered, "I'm so sorry." He forced his wooden legs to move, putting his arm around his friend. "Come into the back. I have a fire going." Rob guided him into the back room and sat him down at the table.

Rob lifted the filled kettle and placed it on the hook over the fire. He knew where Dr. Boylston kept the pewter mugs and the tea. As he got them out, he said, "What are you going to do, Sam?"

"Old Mrs. Newgate has come to care for her. Mother has asked that Martha and I leave the house, in hopes. . ." There was a catch in Sam's voice. "In hopes we will not get sick, too."

"You can stay with us, Sam. You know my mother would want that."

Sam shook his head. "I knew you would be kind enough to offer, but Mr. Campbell and I have already discussed this. I'll be sleeping in the back of the print shop. In fact, I brought a few things there this morning."

Rob made tea and gave Sam a heaping spoon of maple syrup in his, even though he knew the doctor's supply was low. Rob figured Dr. Boylston would agree that Sam needed it.

"Where will Martha stay? Mother would want her to come, even if you can't."

Sam took a long drink of the hot sweet tea and sighed. "She's decided to stay over at Mrs. Newgate's so she'll be close by."

Rob nodded. That made sense.

Sam upended the mug and drank the rest of the tea. "I must go. Mr. Campbell was kind enough to let me come and tell you. I knew you would want to know—and your mother as well." Sam stood to his feet. He seemed stronger now. "Thank you, Rob, for being my friend."

Rob tried to answer, but words failed to come. After Sam left, Rob rinsed the mugs, put things away, and set about straightening and cleaning as much as he could without the doctor's instructions. By the end of the day, the doctor still had not come. Rob expertly banked the fire so the coals would last until morning. Before leaving, he wrote a note to explain to the doctor that the counting house was closed and that he would be there first thing the next morning. He signed his name with a great flourish and many swirls and curlicues.

That evening when he told his family about Mrs. Lankford, Mother wept. Josiah again asked her if she would leave Boston, but she still refused.

Phoebe Lankford died the next week. Funeral bells tolled with such constant regularity, no one knew for whom they were being rung. Hundreds of Bostonians had died since the previous May. Mrs. Lankford's funeral was held at South Church, and all of Rob's family was there. The Reverend Checkley extolled the virtues of the kind and loving woman. Rob fought back tears as he saw Sam attempting to console his weeping sister, Martha.

Outside the church, before they left for the burying ground, Sam took Rob aside. "Rob," he said. "I'm an orphan now, and Mr. Campbell is to be my guardian. Mother never favored the inoculation, so I didn't speak of it much to her. But I've decided now to go ahead with it, and Mr. Campbell agrees."

Rob was incredulous. "You're going to be inoculated?"

Sam nodded. "Then Martha has promised to consider it when she sees how well I fare."

At that moment, Rob made up his mind that he would never let Sam go through with this alone. "When will this take place?" he asked.

"Martha and I must gather a few things in the house to sell to afford the inoculation, but after that I'll be ready. Next week, I believe."

"I'll be right there with you," Rob promised.

"Of course you will, now that you're working with Dr. Boylston."

"I mean that I plan to be inoculated at the same time as you."

"But I thought. . ." Sam glanced over to where Josiah was loading his family into the carriage.

"I'll run away if I have to."

Sam nodded his agreement. "So be it."

Rob and his family returned to the house that afternoon to find

Freegrace in the kitchen weeping. Mother rushed to her and knelt down beside her chair, begging to know the cause of her tears.

"Father is coming this evening to take me. . .," Freegrace said through her sobbing. "They have a place to go to in Salem. Father wants to take my mother and younger sisters and go before the winter storms set in. He insists that I go, too." She dabbed at her tears with a kerchief. The scars on her face were blotchy from her crying. Rob wondered how long she'd sat there crying all alone.

"But of course, you must go," Mother said softly. "You must do as your father asks."

"But I can't bear to leave you. All of you." She looked around at them and burst into tears afresh.

By this time, Rachel had run to her and buried her face in Freegrace's lap, crying uncontrollably. "Don't go away, Miss Freegrace. Please don't go," she begged. Even Thomas had tears in his eyes.

Mother pulled Rachel away and lifted her into her arms. "Don't cry, Rachel. We all love Freegrace, but this parting will be for a short time only. Come, Freegrace, let's get your things ready. Rob, go to the cellar and fetch Freegrace's trunk.

Dusk was gathering as the ox-drawn cart clattered into the back dooryard. Rob didn't remember meeting Mr. and Mrs. Symmes before. They looked to be hard-working, plain farm folk. Josiah went out to greet them and to invite them in for hot cider, but they refused.

"We plan to travel by moonlight," said Mr. Symmes. "Since the selectmen have discouraged travel in and out, we felt it best to go by night."

Mrs. Symmes and the girls were bundled under lap robes atop

the cart and surrounded with bits and pieces of their belongings. It disturbed Rob to think of Freegrace traveling in that kind of discomfort. He and Thomas helped Josiah load Freegrace's trunk, then Freegrace, too, climbed aboard. The large oxen switched their tails and looked about with large, friendly eyes.

"I'm beholden to you for taking such good care of my daughter, Mr. Foy, Mrs. Foy. But I feel compelled to take her to safety. I snatched her from the fire once. I would be foolish not to do it twice."

"We agree with you fully, Mr. Symmes," Mother said, shaking his hand. Then she stepped to the cart and shook hands with his wife.

"We'll bring her back to you safe and sound," Mr. Symmes promised as he leaped up onto the cart.

Before the sounds of the old cart faded in the distance, Rob fled to his room, crying as freely as his little sister. He couldn't bear the thought of their house without Freegrace. He allowed himself to sob and cry until at last he cried himself to sleep.

CHAPTER THIRTEEN
The Bomb

Contrary to Rob's previous plans, he was not allowed to spend
every day at Dock Square. Josiah outlined work for both Thomas
and Rob to do at the house. And now with Freegrace gone, the
boys were called on to help even more. Thomas seemed to seek
out every opportunity to tease Rachel and drive her to tears,
which in turn infuriated Rob.

Josiah went to the counting house each morning, only now

rather than using the carriage, he saddled his own horse to ride. Rob often wondered what Josiah did in the cold, empty building, but he never dared ask. Perhaps his stepfather just walked around and checked on everything.

It took Sam longer than expected to come up with the money for the inoculation. November was nearly half over before he informed Rob that he'd set up the time with Dr. Boylston. It was also decided that he would stay in the room above the apothecary shop until he had recovered from the operation.

Meanwhile, Rob was making his plans to sneak out of the house and join his friend. He packed a few of his possessions in a knapsack and tiptoed down the back stairs. The town crier had just called out that it was two o'clock. The tall clock in the hall agreed. Without Freegrace in her room off the kitchen, it was a simple matter to slip out the kitchen door.

The night was cold and clear. The ground was covered with a few inches of snow that shone in the moonlight. Rob kept his eyes out for the town crier, who was also a constable. At a moment's notice, he was prepared to jump into the bushes and trees at the sides of the road.

Just as he was ready to turn off Salem to Hanover Street, however, Rob heard shouts in the distance. There was trouble somewhere, for he could hear the town crier. He saw no smoke, so it wasn't a fire. He hesitated, wondering whether to go out of his way and investigate. It was of utmost important that no one see him.

Keeping to the shadows of the buildings, he trailed the growing crowd. The commotion was centered on Ship Street near the wharves. Rob was surprised to see they were at the Reverend Mather's house. Fear rose in his heart. The pastor had been under attack as much or more so than Dr. Boylston, due to his support of the inoculations.

Rob crept along next to the houses, trying to get close and yet remain unseen. But no one was paying any attention to him. Presently, amid the clamor, he heard the word "bomb." Someone had thrown a bomb through the Reverend Mather's window!

Two men walked very near to where Rob was hiding. "Too bad it didn't go off," one was saying. "It'd jolly well serve him right for all the trouble he's caused."

"A bungled job for certain. If I'd had a hand in it, the whole house would be an ash heap just now."

Their words became muffled as they passed on by. Rob's heart was thudding in his chest. Someone was enraged enough to try to kill the pastor of North Church. Rob had heard enough. If they did that to a minister, what would they do to Dr. Boylston? Still staying close to the shadows of buildings, he hurried on his way.

At the apothecary shop, he went around to the back, since he knew it was never locked. There was no one about. The fire was banked and the coals were glowing. Since it was still fairly warm, Rob curled up near the hearth to wait.

He hadn't meant to fall asleep, but Dr. Boylston startled him awake as he entered the front door. Rob rose to go meet him. Although the doctor looked very tired, his face brightened at the sight of Rob. "Here so early, Robert? It's only half past three in the morning."

"I'm not here to work today, sir. I'm here to be inoculated along with my friend Sam."

Dr. Boylston strode into the back room and took off his coat and hat and hung them on the hooks. "Does this mean Josiah Foy has changed his mind?"

"No, sir. It just means that I've made my mind up."

The doctor eased down into a chair with a deep sigh. "It's not quite that easy, my young friend. I cannot touch you without Josiah's permission."

"But I've run away. See, I have my things here. I'm prepared not to go home if he won't have me."

The doctor's kind brown eyes studied Rob for a time. "That's a big decision. I know you didn't make it lightly. But the fact remains that Josiah Foy is a powerful man in Boston, Robert. Did you hear about the bomb attack on the Reverend Mather?"

"Yes, sir. I was there just after it happened. I was on my way over here."

The doctor pressed his fingers against his temples. "A terrible, terrible act. They flung a large cannonball filled with turpentine through his window. Had the fuse not been knocked off, it could have destroyed his entire house."

Rob had heard of this type of makeshift bomb. They were used in Queen Anne's War. It was unthinkable that someone would dare do such a thing on the streets of Boston.

"This act shows," the doctor went on, "the level of anger that men have in their hearts just now. We wouldn't want that same anger to take hold of Josiah and cause him to do something he would forever be sorry for."

Rob hadn't thought of the situation in quite that way. "But I want to be inoculated, and I want to be with Sam."

"I understand. And I'm sure the Lord understands as well. I urge you, Robert, to return home and remain obedient to your stepfather. Trust God to work it out."

Going home and admitting he'd run away was going to be extremely difficult. Josiah could even decide to whip him for having done so. "Shall I fix the fire before I go, sir?"

"No need. I'm going home to try to sleep for a time. My mother is there keeping Tommy. Perhaps she'll have a hot breakfast waiting for me." He stood up and stretched his tall frame.

"When is Sam coming?" Rob wanted to know.

"This evening, I believe." As he pulled on his coat, the doctor turned to Rob. "I want you to know I appreciate your belief in me. May God richly reward you for it."

"Yes, sir." Rob opened the back door to leave. "Thank you, sir."

Rob dreaded going home. Wouldn't Thomas enjoy this little episode—especially if Rob received a sound whipping.

The house was quiet when Rob entered through the kitchen door. Soon Mother would arise and begin heating up the bake oven for breakfast. The fire in the large fireplace was still banked from last night. Luck was surely with him. Adjusting the pack on his back, he moved through the kitchen to the back stairs. If he could get to his room, no one would even know he had been missing.

As he put his foot on the first step, he heard soft voices from down the hall. They were coming from Josiah's study. Now curiosity overcame him. Rob set down his knapsack and made his way quietly down the hallway. The closer he got, the clearer the voices became.

Josiah was speaking with a tone of desperation Rob had not heard before. "Mary," he said, "I've asked you to leave before, but now I'm pleading with you. Please go before it's too late. The roads are still passable now, but if a storm moved in, you would be trapped here."

There was a pause as though he were waiting for Mother to speak. After a moment, he continued. "The smallpox scare is only part of it, Mary. There's sure to be more shortages before winter is over and the port is open once again. And now we have demented people throwing bombs. No one knows what might happen."

Again there was quiet. Rob pressed himself against the wall, trying not to breathe. Was his mother going to be leaving? It was one thing to say goodbye to Freegrace, but to his own mother?

"Esther wants you and Rachel to come, and Moseley's ready to drive you. I beg of you to say you'll go. Everything can be made ready by nightfall."

At last Mother spoke. Her voice was clear and steady. "Very well, Josiah, I shall go. Phoebe is gone, and I can no longer help at the village. I need to think of Rachel as well. But I agree to go under one condition."

"Anything, my dear. Anything. Just name it."

"Agree to allow Robert to be inoculated."

Rob sucked in his breath and felt as though he were going to faint right there. He could hardly believe what he was hearing.

"Mary, are you sure?" Josiah asked.

"You said anything. That's all I ask. If Thomas were agreeable, I'd ask for him as well, but I know Robert's heart. He should be at least given that one chance."

How Rob wished he could see Josiah's face.

"I should have known what you would ask," his stepfather was saying. "He's your son, Mary. If this is what you want, it shall be done."

Rob had heard enough. He turned to go but somehow hooked his foot in the rug and almost fell.

"Who's there?" Josiah called out.

There was no getting away now. "Just me," Rob said, stepping into the study.

"Eavesdropping?" Josiah said.

But Mother said, "What in heaven's name are you doing up and dressed at this hour. And with your coat on?"

"I just came in."

"From where?" Josiah demanded. "You've been out and about in the night hours? Don't you know how dangerous that is?"

"I was running away to Dr. Boylston's. But he sent me home. I was planning to be inoculated and then just stay with him in case you wouldn't take me back again."

"Robert." Mother rose and quickly came to him, wrapping her arms about him and holding him close. "Do you see, Josiah? Do you see how strongly his mind is set? And bless dear Dr. Boylston that he wouldn't do this against your wishes."

"Dr. Boylston told me to trust that God would work it out."

"And He has, Robert. He has." She held him to her. Rob relished the moment, knowing too soon his mother would be gone.

The day was spent packing the few trunks that Mother and Rachel would take. They would leave under the protection of nightfall just as Freegrace and her family had done.

Rachel followed Robert about, asking dozens of questions. The one most often repeated was, "Are you coming?" When Robert repeatedly told her no, then she wanted to know why.

"No room, Rachel. Aunt Esther's family is big. There's simply no room."

"You can sleep in my bed."

"There'll be plenty of other cousins in your bed. Besides, we men have to stay here and take care of the house."

Then the tears began to flow. "But I don't want to go away to Aunt Esther's house."

"Don't cry, Rachel. You won't be gone long, and you'll have

other children to play with." He stopped to give her a hug. "And I'll be right here when you get back." Within a short while the questioning began all over again.

Departure time came before Rob was really ready. He never realized how difficult it would be to see his mother and Rachel leave. They gathered around the carriage in the cold night air saying their goodbyes. Moseley lit the lanterns on the front of the carriage, and they cast a golden glow on the snow.

Rob had planned to thank his mother for standing by him. For making it possible for him to be with Sam for the inoculation. But when he tried to talk, no words would come. Instead he clung to her and fought to hold back the burning tears.

"I'm proud of you, Robert," she whispered to him. "Never forget that. I'm very proud of you."

Josiah, however, was unable to fight his tears at all, nor did he try. He held his wife and kissed her and thanked her for agreeing to go, wiping away tears as he spoke.

Rachel, too, was crying. Robert hugged her and lifted her, along with Kitty, up onto the step of the carriage. "Oh wait!" she said. Handing Kitty to Mother, she hopped down, ran over to Thomas, and gave him a hug as well.

"Goodbye, Thomas," she said. "I really do love you." Then she ran back and scurried up into the coach.

Josiah said a quick prayer for their safety, shook hands with Moseley, and suddenly the prancing horses lunged forward and the carriage clattered away into the night.

The house became suddenly dull and dead without Mother and Rachel. Josiah called Robert into his study. He opened his desk and drew out a bag of coins. "This is to pay for the inoculation," he said.

"That's very generous of you, sir, but I'm prepared to work for Dr. Boylston to pay the fee. I know you're opposed to this procedure. You shouldn't have to pay for it."

Josiah paused with the bag in the air, his face grim. "I see." The bag landed back into the desk drawer with a thud, and the drawer pushed shut. "Very well, then. You may go."

Rob ran to his room to grab the knapsack, anxious to be on his way. He hoped Sam hadn't already received his inoculation.

In his room he pulled on his hat and woolen greatcoat, then took down the musket from the hooks. If anything should happen to him, he wanted to have Father's musket right with him.

"Are you worried I'll touch your old musket while you're gone?" Thomas stood leaning against the frame of Rob's doorway.

"That's not why I'm taking it."

"Sure it is. But what does it matter? You always get everything your own way anyway."

"My own way?"

"Sure. You have a special musket from your father, you win the horse race unfairly and get away with it, you're Mother's little favorite in everything—"

"I don't have time to listen to all this. I'm in a hurry." Rob moved toward the door and forcefully pushed Thomas out of the way.

"You take my job at the shipping lines, and now you get to be with your precious old backwoods doctor. See," Thomas called after him as he ran down the stairs, "you get it all. You're a spoiled brat."

Rob ignored him and ran out the kitchen door, hurrying through the icy, still night to the apothecary shop.

CHAPTER FOURTEEN

The Whipping

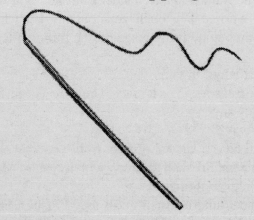

Sam was already at the shop when Rob arrived. "Rob, what're you doing here?" he asked. "Dr. Boylston said you'd been here this morning and he sent you home."

"Where is Dr. Boylston? I thought you would have had your inoculation by now."

Sam shrugged. "He came in for just a few minutes to pick up a few things and told me to wait. So I'm waiting. But you haven't told me why you're here."

The fire was roaring in the back room, and the heat felt wonderful after his cold walk. Rob hung up his things and rubbed his hands by the leaping flames. "I'm with you now, Sam. I have Josiah's permission to be inoculated!"

Sam's face lit up as he slapped Rob soundly on the shoulder. "Hurrah!" he whooped. "Thanks be to God, my friend's here with me. To be quite honest, Rob, fear was beginning to crawl all over me, but now that you're here, it's all gone."

"Fill the kettle, Sam. I'll get the tea and crackers."

As they ate together by the fire and waited for Dr. Boylston, Rob told Sam about his day—how Mother and Rachel were on their way to Roxbury and how his mother had made the agreement with Josiah.

Sam gave a little whistle. "Your mother's a wise woman, Rob."

Rob nodded. Already he was missing her terribly. But no matter how much he missed her, at least he knew his mother was coming back. Sam had no such hope.

After a couple hours, the doctor finally arrived. Now even Rob was getting a bit queasy. But he said nothing. He knew this was the right thing to do.

Rob repeated the story of how his mother had convinced Josiah to give permission for the inoculation. Dr. Boylston smiled. "Didn't I tell you, Robert? It's best to leave the details in God's hands."

"You were right, sir."

Dr. Boylston prepared the needed items, said a short prayer, then asked, "Who's first?"

"I'd like to be, sir," Rob said, mustering up his courage. Sam didn't argue.

The little pricks and cuts the doctor made on his arm didn't hurt much at all. After the pus had been applied, Dr. Boylston applied a cabbage leaf over the sore to protect it. Sam was next. He looked a little pale. Rob wondered if he were going to faint. He hurried to where they'd been sitting by the hearth and grabbed a mug of tea. "You'd better drink this, Sam."

Sam gave a weak smile. "I guess I'd better."

"It's natural to be a little fearful," said Dr. Boylston in his gentle way. After a minute, Sam had bucked up some, and the doctor proceeded. Very quickly, his operation was done as well.

"No one else is staying here just now," Dr. Boylston explained, "so the two of you can look out after one another. You'll sleep upstairs. I'll bring some things for your breakfast in the morning."

"I brought a little food," Rob said, pointing to his knapsack.

"And Martha has agreed to bring things by," Sam added.

"Good." The doctor rose to go. "I'll be checking on you first thing every morning and last thing every evening." He smiled as he pulled on his greatcoat and made ready to leave. "Good night, boys."

The next few days were delightful for Rob. He was where he'd longed to be, and being there with Sam made it even better. Together they cleaned the place, straightened the shelves, and under the doctor's directions, pulverized herbs into powder.

After about a week, Rob's "ripening," as Dr. Boylston called it, arrived. A few sores appeared on his body, but he barely felt a thing. Sam, however, wasn't as fortunate. His sores were more numerous, and he quickly became quite ill.

Rob moved the straw ticking from the upstairs bed down next to the fire so that he could tend to Sam more easily. Dr. Boylston said the more serious reaction might be because Sam had been around people with the pox much more than Rob had been.

The late night hours were the worst. Sam called out for his mother and didn't seem to know where he was. He rolled and tossed about as the fever raged in his body. Rob gently fed his friend and tended to him constantly. Dr. Boylston taught him how to make poultices for the sores and how to apply compresses to reduce Sam's fever.

"I know this looks frightening, Rob," Dr. Boylston said one evening when he'd stopped by. "But believe me, this is mild compared to a genuine case of smallpox."

Rob realized the doctor was trying to set his mind at rest. There had been times in the night hours when Rob wondered if his friend might die. He felt helpless and frightened.

"You're doing a fine job, Robert," the doctor added. "I believe you'd make a fine doctor!"

Those words gave Rob hope and helped him get through the seemingly endless string of days. Martha Lankford brought food by, but Rob kept her outside. If Sam's contact with the disease had worsened his reaction, it stood to reason that she need not be in contact with her brother until he fared better.

Mr. Campbell was greatly concerned about Sam. He stopped by often to check on him and went away shaking his head. "I guess the inoculation isn't as effective as we'd thought," he said at one point.

Thanksgiving day came and went almost without notice. Martha brought a special pumpkin pie for Rob, but he scarcely had time to feed himself because he was so busy caring for Sam. Late in the afternoon, as Sam was sleeping, Rob envisioned his mother and sister sitting down to a table laden with good food, enjoying the gaiety of the holiday. Then he wondered how Thomas and Josiah were making it with no one to cook for them. How long would it be before his family was back together again?

Early one morning, Rob was curled up nearby on a corner of the straw ticking, catching a little sleep. Sam's stirring about woke him. He looked over to see his friend sitting upright.

"Morning, Rob," he said with a silly grin on his face.

"Sam! Sam, you're better," Rob exclaimed. He reached over to feel Sam's face. His skin was cool. The fever was gone. "I can hardly believe it. You were so sick."

Running his fingers through his disheveled red hair, Sam looked around. "I'd almost forgotten where I was. Was it you who took care of me?"

"It was."

"I kept thinking it was Mother. But my mother's dead, isn't she, Rob?"

Rob nodded. "Almost a month ago."

"Now I remember." He shook his head a little. "I think my mind's mixed up. Say, I'm hungry. Got any food?"

"Now that's the best news I've heard in a long time," Rob said jumping up. "Let's eat!"

In a matter of a few days, Sam was well enough to leave. The sores had stopped draining, and his strength had returned. Rob could tell his friend was anxious to get back to the print shop. That was a sure sign of being well again.

Dr. Boylston was all smiles as Sam prepared to leave. "Another success story," he said. "Perhaps you and Mr. Campbell will write this up in the *Boston News Letter*."

"Perhaps we shall, Dr. Boylston." He shook the doctor's hand. "Thank you so much."

"You can thank your friend here. He's the one who took care of you."

"I thank both of you. Together you make a great team." Sam was tying on his muffler and pulling on his coat. "Tell me, Rob, will you be here working now?"

"If Dr. Boylston agrees and Josiah allows me to. At least until the port reopens. That may not be until spring."

"You'll have no argument from me," the doctor quipped.

After Sam left, Dr. Boylston sent Rob home as well. "You've done enough for now. You need to report back to Josiah and let him know how you're faring. If he agrees, I'll see you here tomorrow morning bright and early."

Rob had never been away from home overnight, and here he'd been away for more than two weeks. But without Mother and Rachel at home, he wasn't all that anxious to return. Had the doctor allowed it, he would have stayed at the apothecary shop indefinitely.

Thankfully there'd been a break in the cold weather. The sun was out, and most of the thick snow was melting off the road as he trudged homeward. As he walked up the hill toward the house, he saw a horse and rider coming over Copps' Hill. The rider was pressing the horse to a crazy speed, with the whip flailing the horse all the way.

Poor horse, Rob thought—until he realized it was his horse. It was Abrecan, and Thomas was astride him, beating him!

Fury burned inside Rob like a hot fire. Thomas rode the frenzied horse into the back pasture and up to the stables. Rob cut around the opposite side of the house, laying down his knapsack and musket near the back door. Before Thomas knew what was happening, Rob was running pell-mell toward him.

"Get off my horse! How dare you beat Abrecan like that?"

"We didn't know if you were ever coming back," Thomas said, pulling on the reins to back the horse away. "You could have died for all we knew."

"Well, sorry to disappoint you, but I'm back." With that he reached up to try to pull Thomas off. In defense, Thomas struck him with the whip. Even through his heavy coat, Rob felt the strong sting of the whip. The next time it came down, he fearlessly reached out and caught the end of it, yanking Thomas to the ground with a thud—whip and all.

Wrapping the whip around his palm a couple of times, Rob yanked it from Thomas's grip. Now Rob had the whip and Thomas lay cowering on the snowy ground. With the whip in the air ready to land the first blow, Rob suddenly froze.

Thoughts of Dr. Boylston came to him. The gentle doctor had received endless opposition and unfair accusations, and yet never had he returned evil for evil. With all his heart, Rob knew he wanted to be like that. Suddenly, he threw the whip as far as he could. Turning away, he caught Abrecan's reins and led him to the stable, leaving Thomas lying in the snow.

CHAPTER FIFTEEN

Smallpox Hits Home

Getting along without Mother or Freegrace was difficult if not impossible. None of the three men in the Foy household were worth anything in the kitchen. Cheese and crackers became the fare for most meals, with a little salt fish or cured ham thrown in. Rob thought longingly of how Freegrace would bring up dried pumpkin and apples from the cellar and magically transform them into delectable pies.

Thomas and Rob avoided one another and barely talked. Rob was thankful for every moment he spent with Dr. Boylston away from the house.

In addition to all the other problems, Moseley had never returned from Roxbury. By the second week of December, Rob was certain something terrible had happened. He prayed each day for the safety of Mother, Rachel, and Moseley.

On the days that Rob assisted Dr. Boylston, he took time to hurry to the *News Letter* office to see if a letter had arrived from Mother.

"Not much traffic in and out of the city these days, Robert," Mr. Campbell would say kindly. "Any letter will take a while."

But finally a letter did arrive. Rob ran his finger over Mother's beautiful handwriting on the outside of the folded and sealed paper. He longed to tear it open and relish every word, but it was addressed to Josiah, so he didn't dare.

That evening Josiah called Thomas and Rob into his study to read the letter aloud. Mother and Rachel had arrived safely, but not without mishap. The carriage had skidded off the road on the slick snow, and an axle had broken.

"I should have sent them in the sleigh," Josiah said, shaking his head. "But who knows this time of year? If there'd come a thaw, Moseley would have been unable to return." In the letter, Mother explained that Josiah would need to send a promissory note of payment before the work could begin to repair the carriage.

Rob's heart sank. He was looking forward to Moseley's return—to assist with all the chores if nothing else. Thomas wasn't much with an axe, so most of the wood chopping had fallen to Rob. Since Josiah now had time on his hands, he was at least lending a hand in feeding the livestock.

That night a blinding blizzard swept over the port city of Boston and blanketed everything in layers of drifted snow. As Rob lay snuggled beneath the feather comforters, listening to the roar of the winds, he wondered if things could get any worse.In a few days, he learned they certainly could. Within two days of each other, both Thomas and Josiah came down with the smallpox.

Quickly, and almost without thinking, Robert set things in motion to care for the two patients. He bedded Thomas down in the kitchen near the great fireplace. That way the fire needed for what little cooking Rob did would also warm Thomas.

For Josiah, the study would work best. It was small and easier to heat. All of the other bedchambers were much too large to heat, and Rob wanted both patients to be where he could get to them quickly. When Rob brought the feather ticking from off Josiah's bed to the floor of the study, his stepfather made no complaint.

Now Rob saw what he'd never seen before—fully developed cases of the nightmare disease. It was every bit as terrifying as he'd been told.

For several days there was no thought of sleep. He shoveled out the door to make his way to the woodpile and brought in as many logs as he could. Keeping the fires going was of utmost importance. Making his way to the stable was yet another challenge. He could only shovel a little stretch at a time through the hip-deep snow, then go back in and care for Thomas and Josiah. It took a day and a half to make a path all the way to the stable. He was grateful there was plenty of summer hay stored away for the livestock.

As a result of the blizzard, no selectmen came by to check to see if there were smallpox victims in the house. Day and night,

Rob washed their running sores and applied the poultices. Then he applied cool compresses to bring down the fever and dripped water on their parched lips.

The delirium was the worst. As the fever raged, Thomas and Josiah tossed about and cried aloud. Josiah cried out for Mother again and again. One day Rob was attempting to spoonfeed Josiah a bit of gruel during one of his wakeful moments. Josiah looked at him and said softly, "I've given you little cause to warrant such careful attention as you're giving me."

"With all due respect, sir, I would attend any such person who is suffering as you are."

"Robert," he managed to say in a whisper, "if you'd not had the inoculation—"

"Please don't try to talk, sir," Rob interrupted. He knew what his stepfather was trying to say, but that wasn't important just now. "You need all your strength to concentrate on getting this broth down you."

Thomas's case was much worse than his father's. He wavered between times of hallucinating and being somewhat clear-minded. His sores were more numerous than Josiah's, his raging fever more intense.

Before the week was out, Rob was relieved to see two of the city's selectmen approaching the house in a small, one-horse sleigh. He opened the door to greet them and to report the two cases. He also explained that he was caring for them by himself. "Please get word to Dr. Boylston for me," he said.

"But is this not the home of Josiah Foy?" asked one of the men.

"Yes, it is. What of it?"

"But," the man protested, "I happen to know that Dr. William Douglass is Foy's personal physician."

Rob stood up a bit straighter. Rolling up his sleeve, he produced his scarred arm. "I received this smallpox inoculation from Dr. Zabdiel Boylston," he said with pride.

Both men gaped at the arm.

"Because of this," Rob went on, "I am well today and can care for the sick in this home. Since I seem to be in charge, if only for a short while, I request that Dr. Boylston be notified."

"Yes, yes, young man. We'll see to it. Right away."

Rob's mind was more at ease knowing his friend would soon be there. However, the low supply of firewood concerned him a great deal. That was one thing no one could help with. When the wood was gone, it was gone. There was little wood to be found in the entire city.

That afternoon, as he was changing Thomas's compresses, he realized his stepbrother was weeping. "It's all right, Thomas," Rob said softly. "You're going to be all right."

"I hated you. I hated you." The words came in a parched whisper. "I was the firstborn son of Josiah Foy."

"You still are, Thomas, I assure you. Now don't try to talk."

"Am I going to die, Rob? I'm scared to die. I hated you so much, and now you're helping me." The words sounded mixed up and confused.

Suddenly Rob remembered what Thomas had said the night Rob left to receive his inoculation—something about Rob taking his place. Was it possible that all this time Thomas had been jealous? Had envy been fueling his wretched behavior? Why hadn't Rob seen it before?

"You took my place," Thomas said. "I should have been there."

"Where Thomas? Should have been where?"

135

"At. . .at the counting house."

"Thomas, I didn't want to be there. I didn't want that position."

With great effort, Thomas nodded. "I know. I've watched it. You disdained the very thing I longed for." He was weeping again. "I'm sorry I hated you, Rob. I'm thankful you're my brother. I'm so sorry."

"And I'm so sorry I fought back, Thomas." Rob couldn't stop the tears coursing down his cheeks. But Thomas was once again asleep, and Rob wasn't sure he even heard. Rob prayed anyway, asking the Lord to forgive the two of them for their anger and bickering.

Late that evening, the welcome sound of sleigh bells drew near. Rob met Dr. Boylston at the back door and ushered him into the kitchen.

"I came as soon as I heard," the doctor said. "But I was confident you would be doing a capable job."

He checked on the two patients and was pleased with Rob's nursing. He'd brought more poultices and salves that Rob needed. Then he produced a hamper full of food. "Since I know you're not much of a cook, I thought you could use a few provisions, Robert."

"Thank you, sir. There's been little time to think of cooking, even if I could."

"It's important that you take time to eat. You must keep your strength up to continue your work here."

"I will, sir."

Rob fixed the doctor some hot cider.

"You had friends at the praying town, did you not, Rob?" the doctor said as they sat, resting a moment.

"Yes, sir. Is there word? Is it bad there?"

"Very bad. The Indians have little resistance to the disease. Many have died. You knew the schoolmaster named Patuckson?"

Rob nodded, not daring to breathe.

"Word has come that both he and his son died just before the blizzard hit."

"Neponset," Rob whispered. "Neponset was my good friend." From the pocket of his waistcoat he brought out the bear's tooth. "He gave me this. He told me he had no need of it because he no longer feared death."

"I'm so sorry you lost your friend, Robert. I wish I'd had better tidings to bring you." The doctor drank the remainder of the cider from the pewter mug and then stood. "I must go now, Robert. There's so little time to rest." As he pulled on his coat, he said, "Oh, there is one bit of encouraging news—your new friend Ben Franklin has received his inoculation and is recovering nicely."

Rob smiled. His well-laid trap for Ben had been so senseless. Surely he was learning better. "Please give him my best regards."

"Yes, I'll do that." After giving a few more instructions, the doctor left.

As the door shut behind Dr. Boylston, Rob felt even more alone. That night was the worst for Thomas. He cried out often as he tossed and turned, his eyes and throat swollen from the fever. Rob grieved to see him suffer so. He wished he could do something, but felt totally helpless.

Suddenly, he remembered how Thomas admired the Queen Anne musket. Taking the stairs two at a time, he rushed to his room, grabbed the musket, and came racing down to the kitchen where Thomas lay.

Carefully, he placed it near Thomas so that when the boy woke up, it would be the first thing he saw. "You can touch my musket,"

Rob whispered. "It's all right now. You can even hold it. It just doesn't matter anymore."

Wearily, Rob fixed himself a mug of hot cider and ate some of the tasty meat pies from the basket. Weary to the bone, he propped himself against the side of the warm fireplace to keep watch on Thomas.

Later in the night, a funny little noise woke him. He thought he heard a low laugh. Like a little chuckle. It couldn't be. Was Thomas laughing in his delirium?

Now fully awake, Rob strained to see through the darkness. "Thomas? What is it Thomas?" He felt for the fire tongs and poked at the embers. They flared up, lighting the room.

Thomas was sitting up, cradling the musket, stroking the stock, and giggling. "You put it here. You did this. Silly, wonderful Robert. Your beautiful special musket. You put this here for me."

"Oh, Thomas, your fever's broken." Rob dived into the make-shift bed and hugged his brother. "Thomas, you're going to live. You're going to be all right." Together they laughed and rolled in the bed until Thomas was quite out of breath.

"With all this noise, you'd wake even a sick person," came a voice from the doorway.

"Josiah," Rob called out. "Look here, Thomas is better." Then he realized Josiah was on his feet for the first time in days. "And you're better, too? Whoopee!" he shouted.

Suddenly Josiah was on the bed in the midst of them hugging them both. Rob wasn't sure who was weeping and who was laughing, but it was so wonderful, he didn't really care.

Both of his patients were hungry, so Rob put out plates in the dining room and served food for everyone. Although both Thomas and his father were still very weak, they were able to eat some. It saddened Rob that both of them would now be scarred with pockmarks, but he was deeply grateful their lives had been spared. Before they ate, Rob returned thanks to God.

"How are the animals?" Josiah wanted to know as he ate. "Were you able to care for them and us, too?"

Rob nodded. "The horses and cows are all fine. But the wood supply is terribly low. There may be enough for one more day."

"I'll go down to the wharf presently. Perhaps I can find scraps of wood out behind one of the warehouses."

"I rather doubt it, sir. Dr. Boylston says there's little to be found in the entire city. Besides, you and Thomas still need a great deal of rest." Rob stood from the table and began to clear the dishes away. "Even though you're feeling better, it's important that you rest. As Mother would tell us if she were here, we'll have to trust God."

"Yes, sir, Dr. Allerton," Josiah said with a weak smile.

Before Rob could reply, a loud pounding sounded at the back door. Rob hurried through the kitchen and opened the door to find Moseley standing there with a mammoth armload of wood.

"Moseley! Thomas, Josiah, come quick! Moseley's returned!"

When Moseley saw the still-fresh sores on Josiah and Thomas, his face went ashen.

"It's all right, Moseley," Josiah told him. "We're both fine. Young Robert here was our attending physician and nursed us both back to health."

"Praise be to the Lord God," Moseley exclaimed in a quivering voice.

Rob helped Moseley stack the wood in the firebox and tossed two logs on the fire, watching with joy as it blazed up.

"I pray you'll forgive me, sir," Moseley said as he opened the door and pointed out to the carriage. "But take a look at what I've done."

There was Josiah's expensive carriage with the exquisite satin seats and soft carpeting filled to the brim with dirty, but much-needed, cut wood.

Rob was quiet, holding his breath, certain that Josiah would explode at this ruination of the interior of his fine carriage.

Suddenly Thomas snickered. "It's a fine lot of passengers you've brought back with you, Moseley," he said, peeking around the corner of the door. "But aren't their expressions a bit wooden?"

Then Josiah was laughing as well and slapping Moseley on the shoulder. "Fine job, Moseley. You're a wise man. A very wise man."

"Thank you kindly, sir. And here's something else."

He opened the carriage door and pulled out a large crate from atop the wood. "Here's your Christmas dinner from Mrs. Foy and your sister."

"Christmas?" Rob said. "When's Christmas?"

"Why, poor little laddie," Moseley said, "you've been shut up all these days and lost track of time. Tomorrow is Christmas, Young Robert. This is Christmas Eve."

Rob could hardly believe it. It was Christmas.

"And what a wonderful Christmas it is, Moseley. My life has been spared, and I have my two sons here safe." Josiah put his arms around Rob and Thomas and drew them close. "Merry Christmas, Thomas. Merry Christmas, Robert."

"Merry Christmas, Father," Thomas said.

Robert looked up at Josiah. "A very merry Christmas to you, Father."

Good News for Readers

There's more! The American Adventure continues in *Maggie's Choice*. Twelve-year-old Maggie Allerton is confused. Her friends Dancy Truesdale and Susannah Clarke make fun of the new church movement called "the awakening." They say these unlearned preachers are causing disorder and chaos among the people.

Maggie's close friend Richard Lankford, however, describes the revival meetings as "sweet visits with the Lord." Her older brother Ethan, whom she looks to for wisdom, seems confused as well. How will she learn the truth?

Maggie's confusion is compounded when Susannah is given a slave girl as a Christmas present from her parents. When the young girl Melee is mistreated by Susannah, Maggie wonders how she can help. Then Melee, accustomed to the warm climate of the West Indies, grows gravely ill during the harsh Boston winter. Will Melee's illness aid in leading Maggie to the truth?